They were alone in the silent cavern

"The acoustics here are terrific." Brad's face was in shadow. Then the words of an old Maori love song surrounded her. Was that Brad's voice so low and seductive?

"When I look at you,
You turn your face away,
Though in your heart, dear,
I know you love me."

"Love me..." the words echoed back from the great rock walls around them.

Brad moved close to her, so close that her breath was coming unevenly. "I see what you mean."

He said very low, "Do you, Jacqui?"

"About the echo," she added hastily.

"Who cares about the echo?"

It was no use. A force stronger than she understood was taking over, and suddenly she found herself enfolded in strong, enticing arms, his lips on hers.

Emerald Cave

by

GLORIA BEVAN

Harlequin Books

TORONTO · LONDON · LOS ANGELES · AMSTERDAM
SYDNEY · HAMBURG · PARIS · STOCKHOLM · ATHENS · TOKYO

Original hardcover edition published in 1981
by Mills & Boon Limited

ISBN 0-373-02455-X

Harlequin edition published February 1982

CHAPTER ONE

'YOU'LL be all right, miss?' The middle-aged taxi driver put Jacqui's travel bag down in the dust of the lonely New Zealand roadway. His glance moved to a dilapidated timber cottage, all but obscured by trees, visible up a narrow bush track. 'Your friends are expecting you?'

'In a way!' Jacqui's throaty laugh was infectious. 'My brother's expecting me to turn up some time about now, at least I hope he is! We haven't set eyes on each other for ages and will he ever be glad to see me!'

The driver hesitated, his thoughtful gaze resting on his passenger. A slim girl with vividly blue eyes, a quick warm smile and an air of excitement. He had a daughter of his own round about the same age as this girl, and there was something about Jacqui's youth and enthusiasm that touched him. If she arrived at that derelict-looking place to find no one there, she would be in a bit of a spot, and no mistake!

He said slowly, 'It's fairly isolated up here in the hills. You're sure you wouldn't like me to wait here until you make sure there's someone there?'

'Goodness, no!' Her smile flashed out, lighting up her face. 'There's no need—honestly! If Nick isn't in right now he'll be out working in the paddocks for sure!' Laughter bubbled to her lips with sheer happiness, the effect of the hot sunshiny day, and best of all, the antici- pation of being with Nick once again.

Still the driver hesitated. 'If you're quite sure——'

'Oh, I am! I'll be fine!'

She paid him the fare. It had been a long and expensive journey all the way from Rotorua to this lonely bush track, but what did costs matter? It would be worth every cent of the fare to see Nick. Picking up her travel bag, she

turned off the roadway into a track shaded by overhanging punga ferns and thickly-growing tea-tree, her thoughts
still with her brother. She couldn't wait to see him again!
Family feeling, because he was the only relative she had
in the world? Not really. Somehow Nick had a knack of
making life so much more *fun*! He was five years her senior
and throughout their childhood he had led her into all
manner of adventures, many of which had been downright
dangerous, like the time he had dared her to leap from a
shed roof and she had broken her arm in the fall.

Odd to think that two whole years had slipped by since
she had left New Zealand. Two years since the death of
her beloved parents, when the farm had been sold up.
Because of death duties, there hadn't been a great amount
of money left over from the sale. Jacqui had used part of
her inheritance to visit the village in Kent where her
parents had had their roots. Then had come the novelty of
sharing a flat in London with two other Kiwi girls and
working in a big London office. In all that time she had
received only two communications from Nick. Shortly
after her arrival in England had come a scribbled postcard
from him. He was trying out his luck in the opal fields of
Lightning Ridge, he wrote, before taking a look around
the north of Australia.

Then a year ago, out of the blue, had come a bulky
letter with a New Zealand postmark. Unusual, a letter
from Nick, who never wrote at length. *Unless he happened
to want something*, a dark goblin jeered in her mind. She
thrust the ridiculous thought aside and scanned the page.
'I've bought some land,' Nick had written in his dashing
scrawl. 'A run-off on a sheep station, a bush farm a few
miles from Rotorua. No boiling mud pools on the place,
but there's a trout stream on the property. Not that I'll
have any time for fishing for quite a while, I'll be too
busy getting the place in order.' Odd, the thought shot
through her mind, Nick buying land, for he had never
shown the slightest interest in farming when at home. It
had been a disappointment to their father, she knew.

Maybe he regarded the venture as a good investment.

She brought her attention back to the page in her hand. 'That's the good news. The bad news is that there's a land-hungry guy next door who's taken over the station from the old boy who sold me the run-off. Believe me, this new guy, Bradley Kent his name is, is determined to block me any way he can. He'd give his eye-teeth to get hold of this place. He's keen on trout fishing and would like to get his hands on the stream. As if he hasn't got enough with the thousand acres he runs sheep and cattle on! The greedy beggar has got his knife into me and he's doing his damnedest to give me the push, but not to worry, I know when I'm on to a good thing and he can go chase himself! All I need now is a spot of cash to get the place in running order so that it will bring in some returns next season. And that's where you come into the picture! Luckily the fences are in first-class order and with a little help from your end I can buy some beef cattle, put some sheep up on the hills, fix up the old cottage on the place and make it liveable, all that stuff. You couldn't find a better investment for the bit of cash Dad left you. I'm trusting you not to let me down. Just give me that bit of extra cash and we're in business. What do you say, *partner*? P.S. I've got Pancho here with me and he's looking better than ever.'

Pancho! Her much loved horse that she had left with a girl friend in the country. To think Pancho was on the new farm with Nick—why, that was wonderful news!

She hadn't hesitated for a moment but had dashed off a reply to Nick that very day. 'Of course I'll be in on it with you!' By the same mail she had written to the family lawyer in Auckland asking him to transfer her share of the inheritance from the farm property to Nick. It was as easy as that. That was one of the ways in which they were alike, she and Nick. The enthusiasm for a new project, the impulsiveness. Some folks would term it recklessness, regardless of consequences. All through the following week the sense of excitement lingered. It was happening all over again, Nick letting her in on a new venture. True, the vindictive old sheep station owner up on the hill above the run-off sounded a threatening character, but Nick would find ways of outwitting him, he was clever like that.

Why must she recall right at this moment her father's strong tones? 'Don't you think it's about time you started thinking things out for yourself, lass? Oh, I know you idolise your brother. Nothing wrong in that, but a word of warning, don't you ever give him money. There'll be something for both of you one day when the farm's sold up. I'd hate to see all my hard work bringing in the place tossed away in one of Nick's wild schemes. You look after yourself, lass, never mind about him. Blokes like Nick can look after themselves, they always come out all right.' How could her father have guessed that within a year after that conversation he would lose his life in a tractor accident on his own property? Or that his wife would have passed away only three months later?

She waited impatiently for Nick's reply to her message. It arrived without delay. 'Thanks, Brat. I knew you wouldn't let me down. As soon as I've licked the place into shape you can come out and stay, play at being a tourist at Te Kainga.' With her smattering of the Maori language Jacqui knew the neame meant 'dwelling place'. 'I'll let you know.'

But he hadn't written again and the months had slipped by. Then all at once, in the depths of an English winter, it was the Christmas season once again. Nick's greeting card reached her at the home of an aunt and uncle in London, with whom she was spending the festive period. Just a card with an Auckland postmark. A colour photograph of a typical New Zealand summer scene. Scarlet tassels of the pohutukawa, the New Zealand Christmas tree, overhanging a glimpse of sun-splashed blue sea. 'Love Nick.' That was all. Yet some of the warmth of a New Zealand summer must have got caught up in the folded card, she told herself, for suddenly she was swept by a wave of homesickness. Over on the other side of the world

Nick had a farm of his own—correction, *their* own—that she hadn't yet set foot on. And Pancho was there, her gelding that was the only thing retained from the old farm days.

Rotorua in summertime! Jacqui had a sudden fleeting impression of the high thermal area. Of clouds of steam rising from boiling mud pools a few feet from a busy highway; geysers spraying plumes of steam high against the clear air. She could almost smell the strange sultry odour that pervaded the air.

All the time she had been in England she hadn't felt this way. Maybe she had been too busy enjoying herself, exploring fresh places and making new friends. But now . . . could it be the ending of an unsatisfactory love affair that she had at last put out of her life, that had made her decide to return to her homeland? Fortunately she had retained her return fare in the bank and her travel documents were in order.

Impulsively she dashed off a few words on a New Year greeting card to Nick. 'Hi! Remember me? See you in a month's time at Te Kainga.' He would understand the brief message, being apt to act on impulse himself. All at once she couldn't wait to begin her new life back home in New Zealand. To give Nick more time for his outdoor tasks, she would take over the housekeeping and she would help with the farm work as well.

As the days went by she was a little mystified by a lack of any reply from him, but she told herself that of course there would be some simple explanation for his silence. He could be on holiday in the city. Or maybe in the rush of Christmas mail her blue airmail sticker had become dislodged from the envelope and the card had gone seamail. No matter. It would be fun to surprise him, to catch his expression of astonishment when she met him at the door of the cottage.

Yet now, as she mounted the rotting timber steps leading up to a small open porch, Jacqui couldn't help being taken aback by the state of disrepair of the cottage. Somehow she hadn't expected this—this desolation. The next minute her gaze lifted to the cleared hill paddocks with the neat lines of fencing, the grazing sheep and cattle, and her spirits lifted. Of course, it was clear that all Nick's funds, and hers too, had gone into the improvement of the property, so it didn't really matter if the dwelling were a bit primitive, especially in summer.

It really was an awfully tumbledown-looking dwelling. The paint that had once covered the walls had long since peeled away and long spears of grass straggled over sagging steps. The next moment she caught sight of Nick's red plaid jacket, hanging on a nail in the porch. She recognised the patches she had sewn on to the garment years and years ago. So at least he was here. Pausing in the porch, she waved happily to the taxi driver who, in spite of what she had told him, had continued to wait at the roadside. With a cheerful lift of his hand in response to her signal that all was well, he turned the car in the dust of the roadway and sped away.

Pushing open the door, Jacqui found herself in a rough room containing the bare essentials of living—an old kauri table, two rickety chairs, a shabby couch. In a corner of the room a cardboard carton overspilled with books. The floor was bare, spiderwebs festooned the ceiling and at the uncurtained window a blowfly buzzed against the glass. She flung open the window to let in air fresh with the spicy tang of the pine plantations that covered the hills far above. Then, pushing her way through a sun-rotted curtain, she found herself in a bedroom with a rough bunk bed and a heap of folded grey blankets.

Curiously she crossed the room to examine a faded colour print pinned to the wall. Nick, dark-haired and smiling, just as she remembered him. He was squinting against the sunshine, an arm thrown around the bare tanned shoulders of a blonde girl wearing a blue sunfrock. Nick had always preferred fair-haired girl-friends, she mused. Idly she turned the photograph over and scanned the scribbled words, 'Love, Lorraine.'

She wandered into the kitchen where a torn tea-towel

hung dejectedly from a nail by the sink. The old coal range appeared sadly in need of cleaning. Nick had never been one for housework.

She flung open the back door, to be met by the humming of a myriad insects in the long dried grass all around. Nearby there was a water tank with a basin on a stand and a yellow plastic bucket. In a shed not far away she glimpsed fishing rods stacked in a corner while hanging on the walls were saddles, bridles and horse gear of all descriptions. Clearly there were horses on the property, so Pancho wouldn't be far away. She hurried towards a wide gate and taking care to close it behind her, wandered over grass already dried by the summer sun. In the next paddock a group of steers careered madly in her direction, only to pause abruptly in a black mass, to eye her with interest. Jacqui, however, was used to the curiosity of young cattle and took no notice.

She went on past a patch of ground where blackened stumps were all that remained of trees and the acrid smell of smoke was in her nostrils. Farther up the slope she could see horses grazing, but her piebald gelding was not among them. Not to worry, she turned to retrace her steps, Nick would find Pancho for her when he came home, as he was bound to do before nightfall. Could be he was spending the day in Rotorua township and would come strolling in at any minute, his eyes crinkling in the old familiar way, greeting her with, 'Hi, Brat!'

The thought came unbidden that it was difficult to imagine Nick living in such isolation. He had always been fond of fun and outings, lots of company. But of course she hadn't set eyes on him for ages. He might have changed. Well, she told herself determinedly, he *could*!

Back in the cottage she reflected that what the place needed was a thorough clean up. After all, it was amazing the difference a spring-clean could make. She went into the kitchen and found a broom, bucket and some tatty dusters, and set to work.

Two hours later the place was clean enough to pass

muster—and still there was no sign of Nick.

Jacqui stood hopefully at the door for some sign of life, but the time dragged by. In the end someone did come into sight, a stockman with his dogs, driving a herd of recalcitrant cattle. Watching the horseman pass out of sight around a tree-lined bend, Jackie thought that the road seemed even lonelier than before.

An hour went by, two, three. As she prowled restlessly near the door, Jacqui's gaze was arrested by a sky splashed with fiery-crimson. She had forgotten, away in another hemisphere, the grandeur of a spectacular South Pacific sunset. Long after the glowing golden ball had dropped over the horizon, the aftermath remained, shading pink and lilac into the translucent blue above. When the darkness came the moon rose, flooding the scene with its soft light, softening the stark outlines of the cottage. Jacqui found a kerosene lamp and matches, closed the window where moths dashed against the pane. There were no curtains at the windows, but what did it matter, she told herself, there was no one to see. If only Nick would come!

All at once a sinking feeling in her midriff reminded her that she had not eaten since having a light lunch in Rotorua, and she went to explore the wall safe in the kitchen. She found there an apple, eggs, bacon, a loaf of bread, tea, condensed milk, a jar of coffee. And wonder of wonders, a delectable-looking smoked trout. There seemed to be no supply of staple fare such as flour, bags of sugar, but at least Nick didn't intend to starve himself, even though the amount of food was sufficient for only a night or so. The smoked trout was tempting, but she was determined to wait to share the meal with Nick, for of course he would be back any moment now. So she sipped a mug of coffee and hunched on the couch by the window, munching the apple while she stared out at the moon-silvered scene. She refused to let her mind dwell on depressing thoughts like Nick being away for a few days in town.

When at last she caught the sound of a man's heavy

tread on the path outside, she sprang to her feet, her face alight. 'Nick!' Running to the door, she flung it open, then stood motionless, staring stupidly at the tall masculine figure who was facing her. 'Oh' It took her a moment or so to collect her thoughts. 'I thought,' she said lamely, 'that you were Nick!'

'So you're another one of his girl-friends!' Without any invitation on her part he was actually stepping inside. Of all the nerve! She had an impression of a man in his early thirties, tough and lean and brown with a thin dark face and the coldest eyes she had ever seen. He was taking off his jacket and tossing it down on the couch, for all the world as if he belonged here. 'Well, I've got news for you. He's gone.'

Jacqui was so astonished by his words that she opened her lips, then closed them again. 'G-gone?' she gasped.

'That's right,' he said coolly, and you could tell by the tone of his voice that he had no time for Nick at all.

'But he can't have!' She was speaking her thoughts aloud. 'He was expecting me to come this week. I sent him a message to say I was coming to stay.'

'Too bad. Actually,' the well-shaped lips carved sardonically, 'you don't know your luck! He's taken himself off,' ice dripped in his tone, 'and about time too!'

All at once the penny dropped. Jacqui's blue eyes blazed angrily. 'Now I know who you are!' she burst out accusingly. 'You're that Bradley man, the sheep farmer who sold Nick the run-off.' She squared her shoulders and lifted her rounded chin and tried to look defiant—difficult when he was so much taller than herself. 'He warned me about you! He wrote me all about the treatment you were handing out to him. How you've had your knife in him from the start and would get rid of him if you could——'

He seemed to tower over her. 'And you believed all that? Swallowed it hook, line and sinker?'

'Of course I believed him! He's my brother and——'

'*Brother*?' His assessing gaze swept over her and slowly the disbelief in the grey eyes, veiled by long black lashes, died away. 'It could be true!'

'Of course it's true. And I know Nick——'

'Unfortunately, so do I!'

Jacqui held his glance with her blue accusing gaze. 'So you've got rid of him now, just as you wanted to.'

He shrugged broad shoulders beneath a cotton shirt. 'A matter of business. Your brother agreed to buy the run-off from the previous owner of the sheep station. He paid a small deposit and signed an agreement to pay the balance of the purchase price at the end of twelve months. The time was up when I took over the station, and seeing it was fairly obvious that your brother had no intention of paying a cent more, I put it to him that it was about time he moved on.'

Her eyes blazed into his. 'You would!' Two danger signals flared in her cheeks. 'If Nick couldn't pay you the money he owed you there would be a good reason. I bet he asked you to give him a little more time—don't tell me,' she flung at him, 'I know already. You refused point blank without even listening to him!'

'That's right!'

'There you are, then!' she cried triumphantly, 'you didn't give him a chance! You don't know what he might have done to tide things over until he could pay you.'

Heavy black brows rose sceptically. 'And you do?'

'I told you,' she declared with conviction, 'that I know my brother better than you do.'

He sent her a long level look from compelling grey eyes. He didn't answer. He had no need to, she thought angrily, the sardonic curve of his lips said it all.

'So you just took over the run-off? You didn't give him a chance?

'On the contrary, he had plenty of chances.'

'I don't believe you.' Her voice was unsteady with emotion.

He shrugged his shoulders, but his mouth tightened. 'Believe what you please,' he rasped. 'I have no need to lie to you, whatever story your brother may have cooked up to cover the real facts——'

'You can't get away from it,' she broke in hotly, 'you just took over the place!'

'It was an agreement,' he said inexorably. 'Maybe,' the laconic tones were infuriating to her taut nerves, 'you're not sufficiently up with it when it comes to legal matters to understand the position'.

'Of course I am! I used to work in a legal office.'

He threw her an incredulous glance. 'For how long?'

'For a while,' she murmured evasively. No need to admit to this overbearing character that her legal experience had consisted of two weeks relieving one of the typists. 'Nick wouldn't *do* a thing like that,' she said with feeling, 'he just wouldn't! He'd make an effort to pay something off the debt. He wrote me that he was wrapped up in the place——'

'The property? Or the trout stream that runs through it?'

She recalled the fishing rods stacked in the shed. 'He had to have some recreation,' she muttered evasively.

'Recreation from what? He never did a stroke of work on the place. Look here, you may as well have it straight! When it comes to making any sort of living for himself, your brother Nick is a no-hoper. A year, and what has he done around the place?'

'Plenty!' Her eyes sparkled angrily. 'You can't get away from all that stock grazing up on the hills——'

'I put those sheep and cattle on when I took over the run-off,' he told her with brutal frankness.

But she wasn't beaten yet. 'How about the scrub he burned off in the hill paddock?'

'I sent one of the boys to put a match to it last week.'

She caught her breath. 'When ... did Nick leave here?'

'Two weeks ago. Could be,' he added with deceptive softness, 'that was why he took off in such a hurry. He couldn't face up to meeting that doting young sister of his, the way things look around here.'

'Oh, you!—' she spluttered, at a loss for words. 'Nick knows I wouldn't have cared one bit about my share——'

The words burst from her lips unthinkingly and the next minute catching the glint in his narrowed eyes, she would have given anything to recall them.

'I get it,' he drawled. 'So you were in the big confidence trick your brother played on me too? Well, let me tell you—what's your name?'

'Jacqui—Jacqueline,' she breathed.

'Jacqui's good enough for me. It's all over, the free living, the promises of debts to be paid next year, the lot! My predecessor might have been taken in by your brother's smooth line of talk, but this is a different ball game!'

The two spots of colour faded from Jacqui's cheeks, leaving her very pale. 'You have no right——'

'Believe me, I have every right! I happen to know that your brother borrowed money from the trusting old boy who was running the station when I took over. A fairly hefty sum that Nick hadn't the slightest intention of ever doing anything about.'

'How can you say that?' she flung at him. 'It's a lie.'

His cold grey eyes met her accusing glance. 'It's the truth——'

'So *you* say!'

A dark flush mounted to his cheeks and she felt his strong hands on her shoulders. 'Now look here—what's your name? Jacqui——'

'Take your hands off me!' She wrenched herself free of his grasp.

Immediately his hands dropped to his sides and he stood very still, only his eyes alive and glowing with anger. 'Okay, okay, seeing you're paranoid about your brother, I can see I'm wasting my time trying to get through to you. Let's drop it, shall we?'

She scarcely heeded his words, she was so incensed. How dared he, how dared he insinuate that Nick was lazy and untrustworthy—worse, that he was a cheap confidence trickster. 'He did try to make a go of things,' she defended hotly, 'what about those trees cut down up on the hill? That was something, wasn't it?'

'You reckon?' His lazy drawl cut like a knife. 'I felled that lot myself, after your brother cleared out.'

She all but choked with anger and frustration. 'Just because I wasn't here, you think you can blacken Nick's character as much as you wish. Well, you won't! Not with me!' Her eyes, of an intense blue with a darker ring around the iris, sparkled through a mist of tears. 'You're making it all up——'

'And why,' his tone was cuttingly soft, 'would I do a thing like that?'

'How would I know?' she demanded angrily, 'how would I know *anything*! I only hear what you choose to tell me, and Nick has warned me about you. He said——' She broke off, for his expression was so forbidding that instinctively she shrank back. In the tension-charged atmosphere the thought slid through her mind that she knew nothing of this man. He was a stranger to her and she was here alone with him, very, very much alone. Were he to become violent there would be no one to heed her cries for help.

Something of her panicky thoughts must have got through to him, for all at once she saw his clenched fists relax. The silence seemed to Jacqui to go on for ever, then he muttered. 'It's up to you.' Why did she get the impression that it had cost him considerable effort to restrain himself from physical retaliation against her?

Moving to the doorway, he stood looking out into the moonlit scene, thumbs hooked in the belt of slim-hipped jeans.

Jacqui ran the tip of her tongue over dry lips. If he could show restraint, then so could she. Forcing her voice to a matter-of-fact tone, she said, 'I suppose you left Nick without a cent to his name? That's what you wanted, wasn't it?'

He swung angrily, a muscle jerking in his cheek, and

once again she realised she had gone too far. 'Apparently,' he observed with studied irony, 'he had sufficient funds to take him and his girl-friend to Canada, or so the story goes.'

'You don't *know* that!' she flung at him. 'You admit yourself that it's only a rumour.'

Once again he shrugged the accusation aside. 'Please yourself what you believe.'

'I will! What's the use of listening to you when you do nothing but tell me lies!'

'Lies! Now you listen to me——' All at once she realised he was looming over her, so close she could feel his breath on her face. Then for the second time that night, she felt the painful pressure of strong hands on her shoulders.

'Go on!' she gasped, 'bruise me! If you think you can make me change my ideas about you——' Her voice died into silence because something strange was happening, as if the air was suddenly charged with electricity and currents were rushing wildly through her, so that she couldn't . . . think . . . straight. With a sense of surprise she realised she was trembling, and that too was odd, for in spite of his tight-lipped fury, somehow she was no longer afraid of ill-treatment at his hands.

'Sorry.' She barely caught the muttered word and over the wild tumult of her senses she felt his hold slacken. She slanted a glance towards his closed, set face, but his expression remained unreadable.

In an effort to calm herself she drew a deep breath and tried to act as though nothing untoward had happened between them. 'What about Pancho?' she enquired, in a voice husky with emotion. 'My horse? Nick said he had him here. I suppose,' she said very low, 'you've sneaked him away from here as well as everything else?'

In the angry silence she thought she had at last scored a victory over him. Then: 'I'd sure know you two were brother and sister——' he drawled mockingly.

'Yes, we are alike, aren't we?' she cut in in an endeavour to forestall mention of the unpleasant characteristics he was no doubt about to enlarge upon. 'Everyone says the same,' she agreed silkily. 'The same black hair and blue eyes——'

'I wasn't thinking of appearances.' How, she wondered, could such a simple remark be so loaded with menace?

She was feeling so *mad* with him, but she made an effort to speak calmly. 'All I'm asking you is what happened to Pancho when you grabbed the bush farm back from my brother?'

'If you mean,' he corrected meaningfully, 'when the property reverted by law to me, the answer is yes. I have the horse at my place.'

'You would,' she said bitterly. 'You wouldn't miss the chance of a good mount like Pancho. You'd only have to take one look at him to know——'

'You're way off beam there,' he said quietly. 'When I came across him a few days ago, he'd been running wild in the bush, must have been up there quite a time, going by the wounds and torn skin that will be quite a time healing up.'

Jacqui faced him angrily. 'Nick wouldn't let him run wild in the bush——'

His lip curled scornfully. 'Not if he were away in town for months at a time?'

'He wouldn't *do* that,' she defended heatedly, 'not with the stock——'

Thick black eyebrows lifted ironically, 'What stock?'

'Are you telling me,' she said slowly, 'that Nick had no stock at all, nothing but Pancho?'

'I'm not telling you,' he corrected smoothly. 'It happens to be the truth. Oh, he had a few head of mangy beef cattle at the back of the run that I took over when he left.'

'I'll bet you did,' she said in a low tone. 'You're just saying all this,' she flung at him, 'to protect your own interests! I know you're making it all up——'

'And I know,' he grated, 'that you're about as un-realistic and plain stupid as that brother of yours you set such store by!'

All at once the black tide of anger she had been trying to keep under control mushroomed up in a blind fury and she slapped her hand hard across his sun-weathered cheek.

Feel better now?' Those steely grey eyes seemed to be boring into her. 'If you don't believe me, you're welcome to come over to the homestead and see for yourself.'

She swallowed, said huskily, 'You know you're quite safe saying that. I bet you were responsible for the condition Pancho's in. You blame everything on to Nick,' she went on in a low voice thick with emotion. 'Just because he isn't here to speak for himself.'

'You're doing a fairly good job of defending him,' he drawled drily. 'When it comes to sticking up for a no-hoper, he couldn't do better himself!'

'Oh, *you*——' She shot him an angry, indignant look, and to her horror felt the tears spill over on to her cheeks.

He sent her a long-suffering glance. '*Now* what's the matter? If it's your horse you're worrying about——'

'Of course it is!' she cried crossly. 'You don't think I'd be worrying about myself, do you, even though Nick and I were partners. I don't care about the mon——' She stopped short, for what would this unfeeling male care about her share in the venture? Nick would explain about the money she had sent him, of course he would. There'd be some simple reason for all this.

His eyes, strange eyes that seemed so full of light, were beamed full on her face. 'What was it you were going to say?'

'Nothing. Nothing that matters,' she murmured hastily. 'Forget it.'

'Well, now that we've got Nick's problems sorted out——'

She shot him a taunting look. 'Have we?'

He ignored that. His next words took her by surprise. 'I'll rustle up something to eat.'

Jacqui hunched a shoulder. 'I'm not hungry.' That

would be the day, when she would share a matey meal with him!

He strode into the kitchen and soon she heard him whistling a tune. Whistling! Just as though having ruined all Nick's chances of making a living for himself here were a nothing thing. But of course, with all his hundreds, perhaps thousands, of productive land, what would he care?

He put a match to the fire already laid ready in the coal range and soon he placed a blackened kettle over the roaring flames.

Jacqui eyed him moodily as he slapped down a loaf of bread on the table and began cutting slices and spreading them with butter. A few minutes later he carried in two plates, each with a portion of smoked trout. Jacqui stared at the food vindictively. I wish I'd eaten it all before he got here, she thought. That might have taken that self-satisfied look from his face!

He made a pot of tea and poured two mugfuls. If he had asked her she would have refused the drink, but he pushed the mug towards her, and with a brief 'thanks' she sipped the hot liquid.

'Bread?' All at once she was feeling hungry.

'Oh, all right, then.' She told herself there was no sense in starving herself just for the sake of someone she would never see again. She helped herself to a thick slice of wholemeal bread and tried to ignore the derisive glance of the man seated opposite her at the table.

The smoked trout with its smoky aromatic tang looked more than appetising, but pride forbade her changing her mind, so she watched as he consumed his portion, apparently with relish. Clearly destroying other people's hopes didn't spoil his appetite one little bit, far from it!

CHAPTER TWO

'You may as well have this,' he was extending the plate of untouched food. 'No sense in wasting it. Guaranteed to be freshly caught and smoked.'

Weakly Jacqui gave in and took the plate from him. The fish was delicious, with a faint smoky flavour of the tea-tree firing used in the smoke-house.

'Nick went trout fishing too, you said?' She spoke unthinkingly and at once knew she had made a dreadful mistake, for the mocking glint was back in his eyes.

'All the time. You could say that was about all he did do during the time he was here.'

Abruptly, Jacqui pushed her plate aside. 'You never let up on him, do you?'

'Don't let it spoil your meal,' he advised curtly. 'You don't believe what I tell you anyway. Isn't that what you keep telling me?'

Frantically she searched her mind for a cutting response, but all she could come up with was an indignant, 'That's true, I don't!'

'While we're on the fascinating subject of your brother,' he was pouring himself a second mug of tea, 'there's just one thing I'd like to get straight.'

She eyed him challengingly. 'And that is?'

He met her gaze with those lively, full-of-light eyes. 'Just where do you come into Nick's business schemes, financially I mean?'

She lifted her rounded chin. It was a gesture she was doing a lot of tonight. 'If you really want to know——'

'Oh, but I do.' His bland enquiring look was infuriating.

'We were partners in the property.' She rushed on, eyeing him defiantly. 'Nick bought the land and I provided funds for the stock. Satisfied?'

'Not quite. He sent her a considering glance. 'It does make one wonder what happened to your contribution, though of course two air tickets to Canada would——'

'You've no need to concern yourself about my affairs.' She was finding it difficult to keep her temper in check. 'Nick will have paid me back my share of it, every cent. I've only got to contact our lawyer——

'You do that,' the laconic voice cut across her throbbing tones. 'After all, you'll have to face up to facts sooner or later—finish your fish!' he commanded in a no-nonsense tone.

'No!'

He shrugged broad shoulders. 'Okay then, please yourself.'

He completed his meal in silence, then cleared away and washed the dishes in the sink. Jacqui didn't offer to help him, she simply remained at the table, waiting until he came back into the room.

'I suppose,' she said pointedly, 'that you'll be going soon?'

'Going?' He stared at her uncomprehendingly. 'Going where?'

'How should I know?' A dreadful suspicion was forming in her mind, but she spoke airily. 'Back to your own home, I suppose,' and discovered she was holding her breath for his answer.

'Tomorrow's time enough.' He spoke carelessly as he bent over the carton of books. Picking up a paperback, he flicked through the pages. 'If you're wondering why I'm here——'

She was, but she had no intention of giving him the satisfaction of admitting so. 'Not really.'

Ignoring her comment, he tossed the paperback aside and picked up a hardback novel. 'I had to go to a horse sale up country in this direction, so I made a stop at the bush farm here on my way back. I wanted to check on the fences anyway——'

'I suppose,' she cut in recklessly, 'you didn't trust Nick

to keep them in order?'

He threw her an ironic glance. 'How did you guess?' He broke the angry silence. 'For your information, Jacqui, I've no intention of travelling any farther tonight just because you've taken it into your head to move into my cottage.'

Jacqui bit her lip. Her thoughts were on the single bed in the bedroom, but she was determined not to reveal her uneasiness in that direction. 'If you won't go,' she said spiritedly, 'then I will!'

'That's an interesting thought.' He eyed her with his cool enquiring glance. 'Where will you go?'

'I don't know . . . somewhere.' She avoided his glance. 'There must be a house around here where I could use a phone, order a taxi to pick me up and take me back to Rotorua.'

'There isn't, you know.' He seemed to be entirely uninterested in her sleeping arrangements.

She stared at him in disbelief. 'You're just telling me that. You want to keep me here——'

The moment the words had left her lips she regretted having spoken.

'*I*—want to keep you here?' She squirmed mentally beneath his innocent stare. 'Whatever could have given you that idea?'

She tried to drag her thoughts together and in an endeavour to cover her slip of the tongue, said with mock bravado, 'Well, the way you're acting. You're not helping me to get somewhere else to stay for the night, are you?'

'Me?' The thick black eyebrows rose enquiringly. 'What can I do? This place is well on the road to nowhere!'

She bit her lip distractedly. 'There must be somewhere else.'

'There isn't, you know.' He was picking up books from the carton and glancing idly through them before discarding them. 'If you don't believe me, take a look outside. You won't see any lights and that's for sure.'

She had already figured that out for herself, and had to admit that just for once, he was speaking the truth.

'You're welcome to make use of this place.' He spoke carelessly and she threw him a swift glance from under her eyelashes, but he appeared to be intent on the book he held in his hand.

'I'll tell you one thing,' the quietly cutting tones broke across her tumultuous thoughts. 'You've nothing to fear from being here with me.' Jacqui reflected that from the tone of his voice you got the impression that he wouldn't as much as come near her with a ten-foot pole, not if he could help it. Of course she was relieved at his lack of interest in her. Lack of interest? It was downright dislike. Yet his obvious aversion to her was definitely deflating to her ego. For this wasn't in line at all with the reaction she was accustomed to of a newly met male acquaintance. Even if you hadn't been told so many times, you couldn't help but know if your eyes were an intense shade of blue and folk, especially menfolk, seemed to be attracted to her smile. Come to think of it, her smile was something that this particular man hadn't seen. Not that she wanted to be on friendly terms with him, heaven forbid!

His lean good looks and vibrant air of aliveness and strength belied his real character, but even so there was something offputting in being treated as if she weren't here at all.

'What's wrong?' he enquired coolly. 'If you're worrying about being here for the night with me, forget it!'

'I'm not!' she flashed. But she was, and he knew it. Beyond an ironical glance however, he said no more but slipped the book in his pocket and strode towards the bedroom. He emerged almost at once, a grey army blanket hanging over his arm.

'I'll doss down on the couch,' he said carelessly. His cool stare raked her mercilessly. 'You won't need to check if there's a key in the lock!' Somehow, Jacqui thought crossly, he managed to make the words sound more in the nature of an insult rather than a reasssurance.

There didn't seem anything further to be said, so without anwering him she went into the bedroom, closing the door

behind her. Immediately she found herself in total darkness.

'Candle and matches in a box by the bed!' came a
masculine voice through the door, and after a certain
amount of groping she found both articles. Trouble was
she had difficulty in striking a match because of the stupid
trembling of her hands.

'Found them?' came the voice again, and at that
moment to her relief, the wick flared into life. 'Yes.'

'Right!' She was holding her breath, her ears alerted to
the slightest sound. She had forgotten, during her sojourn
in London, the intense stillness of the New Zealand
countryside. Somewhere up in the hills a sheep coughed,
a night owl echoed its plaintive cry on two notes: More-
pork, more-pork. Through the uncurtained window a star
fell from the roof of the sky. At last as no further sound
came from the adjoining room, she undressed, slipped into
cotton pyjamas and crawled into bed, pulling a blanket
over her, although she scarcely had need of it in the
summer night. For a long time she lay wakeful, but at
last her tense muscles relaxed, she blew out the candle
and despite all her apprehensions, drifted into sleep.

Next morning when she surfaced from sleep the sun's
rays were streaming over the pillow and for a few moments
she lay still, puzzled by her surroundings. Then the events
of the previous day came rushing back to mind and she
lay tense, listening for sounds from the next room. None
came, however, and getting out of bed she went to the
window to catch sight of a horseman moving along a rise.
Bradley Kent, patrolling his fences, and goody, goody, far
away from the cottage at the moment. With a bit of luck
she would be up and dressed and have had her breakfast
before he returned. For all at once she was feeling raven-
ously hungry, due no doubt to the fresh country air and
her own stubborn refusal to complete her meal the previous night.

Never before had she dressed in such haste, pulling on
panties and bra, thrusting over her head a cream-coloured

knit top over scarlet slacks. A comb run through her hair, a quick splash in the bathroom, then she was hurrying into the kitchen. There luck was with her, for the fire was crackling in the range and a blackened kettle was singing over the flame. She found a frying-pan and soon egg and bacon were sizzling and an appetising aroma of coffee filled the room. She almost made it too, but just before she had finished her meal, she caught the clatter of hoofs in the yard. He must be riding a racehorse, she thought resentfully, to have arrived back here so quickly.

'Smells pretty good.' He had come in after washing himself at the outside tap, dark hair still damp where he had run a comb through it and those too-perceptive grey eyes on her face.

If he expected her to leap from her seat and start cooking his breakfast, Jacqui told herself, he was in for a surprise.

'Any eggs left?' he enquired pleasantly.

She didn't trust the apparently friendly enquiry, for experience had taught her that his affable comments inevitably conveyed a hidden barb, like suggesting she had consumed five eggs for her breakfast. Aloud she said defensively, 'Of course there are! One's enough for me.' Belatedly she remembered that it was his food she was talking about. Oh darn! Why did it have to be his house, his food? She drew a deep breath.

'Don't worry about me,' he was saying, 'I'm used to looking after myself.' He was busy at the stove.

'I wasn't going to anyway.' She attempted to finish her meal, but it was difficult to eat nonchalantly beneath his ironic gaze. The minute his back was turned she bolted down the food on her plate, only to choke on the hot coffee that burned her throat.

She was just about to leave the table when he dropped down to seat himself opposite her. 'Have you decided what you're going to do today?' He eyed her enquiringly over the rim of his coffee mug.

'About what?' She didn't trust him one little bit.

'Making your escape from here?' He knew how she had felt about him last night, the thoughts flashed through her mind. He had understood only too well that needless apprehension of hers of being forced to spend the night alone with him in the loneliness of the outback. With an effort she forced her voice to a casual note.

'What would you suggest?'

He shrugged. 'Over to you, that one. Either I leave you here and ring from the homestead to order a taxi to take you back to Rotorua or——'

Jacqui wondered what was coming. There would be nothing in any way appealing about any alternative arrangement he might suggest, that was for sure.

'If you really want to see your horse——'

'I told you I do!'

'And I told you that you're welcome to look him over and see for yourself how he's getting along. I got the feeling you had a soft spot for him, so if you're really concerned——'

'Of course I'm worried over Pancho!' She was playing for time. After a moment or so she said slowly, 'You're asking me to come with you to your place?'

'That's right.' His voice was deadpan. 'Stay for a while if you want to, until you're satisfied your horse is on the mend. There's swags of room.'

She eyed him suspiciously. 'Why are you inviting me over there? You know you don't really want me around!'

He eyed her with his impassive stare. 'Nor do I particularly care for having my word doubted.'

'Well . . .' She hesitated.

'Oh, for Pete's sake!' Once again his explosive feelings flared. 'If you're back on that tack, you can forget it! I can assure you,' his tone was cuttingly soft, 'you'll be in no danger from me. There's a houseful of bods at Waiwhetu—housekeeper, relations, staff, the lot!'

To her chagrin Jacqui felt the hot colour flood her cheeks. The man was a mind-reader, damn him! Just one more facet of his unpleasant personality.

'Well, make up your mind.'

There it was again, the challenging glint in his eyes, and because she couldn't bear to let him get the better of her, she decided to take up his offer. She sent him a glance from under her lashes. 'Just to see Pancho, of course?'

Sarcasm was wasted on him. He simply ignored it.

'I'll think about it.'

'*Think about it!*' He bent on her his deep compelling glance. 'Look, I'll be on my way out of here in thirty minutes flat, so are you coming with me or not? It's all the same to me.'

All at once her mind was made up. 'I'm coming.'

'Right!' Pushing back his chair, he gathered together the empty plates and carried them into the kitchen. Then he went out of the door, whistling a tune as he moved down the pathway. He was a great one for whistling, she mused resentfully, and no wonder, seeing he contrived to get his own way by riding roughshod over the feelings of other people. If only he weren't so attractive, with his dark good looks and male magnetism. Determinedly she thrust from her mind the chaotic feelings sparked off by his closeness last night. She mustn't ever risk that sort of encounter again!

As she ran water into the sink she could see him brushing down his mount, then he led the stock horse back to the hill paddock.

A little later she had zipped up her travel bag and tidied up the kitchen and was taking the food from the safe when she realised he was standing in the doorway regarding her, his face set and unsmiling. 'It won't work, you know.'

She stared up at him uncomprehendingly. 'Do you mean you want the food to stay here?'

'I mean the helpful little housewife bit.'

'*What!*' Her blue eyes were blazing. 'If you think I'm trying to get around you——'

'I'm just warning you, don't bother trying, that's all.'

'Well, of all the nerve——' She was so angry she

banged down a bag of eggs on to the sink bench and to her horror saw broken eggs running from the bench down to the floor beneath. The amused quirk of his mouth didn't help any. She faced him accusingly. 'Now look what you've done! I'm only asking you, do you want this food put away again or——'

He shrugged carelessly. 'Throw it in the back of the car. There's a carton in there somewhere—I'll get your bag.'

'It's in the bedroom.' She was still so furious she could scarcely bring herself to speak to him. If it weren't for Pancho she would never be leaving here in his company!

'So you've just got here by air from England?' He was coming out of the bedroom, her travel bag in his hand. 'Been out of the country long?'

'Two years,' she said shortly.

'Quite a time,' he murmured in his deceptively soft accents, and once again Jacqui realised she had fallen into a trap. His next words confirmed her suspicions. 'Long enough for you to have been out of touch with what's been happening over in this part of the world!'

Her cheeks flushed with anger, she flung around to face him. 'If you're getting at Nick again . . .'

Without even troubling to listen to her, Bradley Kent was moving out of the door to stow her travel bag in the trunk of the vehicle. I hate him, she thought. I'd do anything to get even with him for what he's done to Nick. Deep down in her mind a tiny voice of truth piped up. *And for the way he's treating me!* Just give me a chance, she vowed, throwing the matter over to fate, one chance to get even with him and I'll do the rest!

It was the strangest, most silent journey that she had ever experienced. Seated as far away as possible from her companion, she stared out of the open window and prayed that the homestead wouldn't be too many miles distant.

A pity it had to be this way, she reflected, because the countryside through which they were passing was a delight. They sped over hills thickly covered with green native bush while in the distance plantations of pines were a serrated line etched against the incredibly clear sky. Once or twice Jacqui just stopped herself in time from an involuntary exclamation. For as they swept to the crest of a hill she caught a glimpse of a calm blue lake where tall trees met their reflections in the tranquil depths below. She almost cried out in delight, but a glance towards the impassive face of the man at her side was sufficient to make her bite back the words that trembled on her tongue. For clearly he had no intention of making the journey anything in the nature of a sightseeing trip. He had tossed off an offer to take her to see Pancho and that was it. Apparently the invitation, if one could call it that, did not include any such human qualities as everyday remarks or even polite conversation. If that was the way he wanted it, it was okay with her! Nevertheless, it was a strange feeling to be here on this sunshiny champagne day with a man who despised her, a man whom she couldn't stand at any price. You wouldn't think, her thoughts wandered as they sped up a dusty track, to look at him ... In spite of all she knew of him she had to acknowledge that the dark forceful face had something— all at once she realised the direction in which her thoughts were drifting and pushed the betraying thoughts away.

She had been so careful all this time not to make some pleasant remark, and then when they were nearing the end of the journey, she had to spoil it all. They had been speeding up hills on a tree-shadowed road and then dropping down into gullies where the lacy green of giant tree-ferns starred the darker native bush. Then, as they came over a rise, she found herself gazing over cleared hillsides where grazing sheep were dotted as thickly as daisies. High on a hilltop, screened by towering native trees, she caught a glimpse of a mellow brick home and farther down the slope, the reddish timbers of a woolshed. Soon she could see the stables, garages and stockyards. A white-painted timber bungalow was doubtless the home of a married shepherd employed on the vast station. It was like a small village.

'The brick home with its shelterbelt of trees,' the words sprang to her lips unbidden. 'It's so beautiful.'

'Think so?' Something in his tone drew her sideways glance and she saw that his expression had kindled and a look of pride had leaped into his eyes.

The next moment realisation flooded her. 'It's your home, isn't it?'

'That's right.' His tone was as laconic as ever, but he was too late, he had already betrayed his feelings. One up to her!

Presently they swung into a wide entrance and as they clattered over a cattlestop Jacqui's gaze went to a wea-thered sign with its Maori name printed in faded black lettering.

Bradley Kent must have followed her upward glance. 'Waiwhetu,' he told her, and added briefly, 'Don't ask me what it means.'

'*I* know,' Jacqui said smugly, for years ago she had picked up a little of the Maori language. 'Actually, it's "star water". Something to do with the lake around here, I expect, and reflections at night.' She couldn't resist the temptation to air her knowledge. '*Nga kanohi o te rangi.*'

He maintained an annoying silence.

'The eyes of the sky'—that's the Maori way of describ-ing stars.'

'Is that so?' His tone was off-putting, but Jacqui didn't mind. At least, she thought with satisfaction, she had proved to him that he didn't know everything!

Now above them she could see clearly the rambling house with its long verandah running the length of the building. Spacious lawns sloped away from the dwelling. There were tennis courts at one side and steps led down to the blue waters of a swimming pool, screened by blossom-ing bushes.

The small victory she had scored over him must have gone to her head, she mused, for she no longer cared whether or not he made any reply to her comments. Her gaze lifted to the long flower borders edging the stretches of lawn. Even from a distance she could glimpse the colourful blossoms that were probably roses and petunias. 'All those flowers,' she marvelled. 'Goodness, someone here must work awfully hard in the gardens!'

His tone was discouraging. 'I have a man who takes care of the grounds and garden, an old shepherd who's been at Waiwhetu for most of his working life.'

'All that time?' She eyed him mockingly. 'With you?'

'That's right, with me.'

She shook her head in mock surprise. 'You must pay him a hefty wage.'

He ignored the underlying sarcasm in her words. 'He doesn't complain.' Once again she threw him a sideways glance, but his impassive face gave nothing away. He vouchsafed no information about his home but left it to her to make her own observations.

There was no doubt, she reflected, that the station was on a big scale. All these farm buildings, the tractors and machinery she glimpsed in sheds, the hills behind rising range upon range to fade into the blue distance. Anyone could see that the hill country had been brought into production. She wouldn't mind betting that once it had been bush-covered, but now the fern and scrub had been cleared away and the land made fertile with the help of fertilisers sprayed from top-dressing planes. This was the home of a wealthy landowner—her lips tightened—and with all this he had deliberately ousted Nick from his modest bush farm. She would never forgive Bradley Kent for the way in which he had treated Nick, never!

They were passing the stockyards now and above the dust rising around the milling steers, a man mounted on a big roan horse raised a stockwhip in greeting. A moment later, when she glanced back, he was still staring after the car. Her lips quirked at the corners. At least that particular young man had displayed a flattering reaction at sight of her. Or maybe, she reflected wryly, he was merely curious as to the strange girl the boss was bringing home with him after his trip to the horse sale up-country. If only the young stockman knew the true circumstances of the meeting!

'My brother Rick.' She realised she was being favoured with a few words.

They sped past the outbuildings and soon they were sweeping past a white timber bungalow. At a clothes line at the back of the dwelling a young woman was pegging out baby clothes. Jacqui guessed that this home, like the other one they had seen, belonged to a member of Bradley Kent's staff. The next moment she forgot everything else, even her feelings regarding the man seated beside her, for in a paddock on a rise she caught a glimpse of grazing horses. Eagerly she peered at the animals, but there was no piebald among them. 'Where is he—Pancho?'

'Not with that bunch. Those are the brood mares. I'll take you to his paddock.' Clearly he was anxious to get rid of her just as soon as possible, and that was fine with her. All she wanted of him was to see her horse.

He turned into a rough track and they bumped up a rise. Presently he was slowing to a stop near a wide gateway and Jacqui leaped out to open the gate and close it when the car had gone through. Funny, she thought, getting back into the vehicle, how soon one reverted to the old habits of farm life and the unwritten law that it was the duty of the passenger to see to the gates.

A brief 'Thanks', and they were lurching higher up the rise. A second gate to open and shut, then Bradley Kent braked to a stop. A few minutes later they were in a big paddock. 'Come on!'

He was striding over the sun-dried grass and she hurried along to keep pace with his long strides. 'I don't see him——'

'Over there, in the shelter of the trees!'

She ran ahead towards a cluster of tall rimu and totara trees, then stopped abruptly, gazing uncertainly towards a piebald horse that was half hidden in low growing bush.

This couldn't possibly be her proud, spirited show-jumper, this pathetic-looking animal with long matted coat and lacklustre eyes. It was as if his whole body had shrunk. At that moment the horse caught sight of her. He gave a whinny and came limping towards her. 'Oh, Pancho, what's happened to you?' Tears misted her eyes as she cradled the mud-caked head in her arms. For there were festered wounds on his flanks, long open cuts from which the skin hung loose, overgrown hoofs. The animal must have been alone for quite a time for him to be in this state of semi-starvation. There'd been some hideous mistake, of course. Nick would never have left Pancho on the bush farm to fend for himself. All at once anger mushroomed up inside her and she flung herself around, eyes blazing accusingly, to face the man standing silently at her side. 'He's in a terrible state!'

'What would you expect?' His eyes were flint. 'When I came across him he was hung up in supplejack in the bush. I had to cut it to set him free. You can see the hair and skin worn off his shoulders and hips where he'd been thrashing around trying to get out. Lucky for him I happened to come along that day or he'd have starved to death.'

She shuddered. 'Don't!'

'It's true.'

This time she couldn't dispute his words. Pancho's skinny, emaciated frame was evidence enough. All the same—'Why hasn't the vet seen to him?' she demanded, her voice thick with emotion.

'He'll be along. Your Pancho will be okay, don't worry——'

'*Don't worry!*' The wind on the hills tossed her hair across her eyes and she flung the dark strands back from her face impatiently. 'How can you talk like that! Letting him be in this dreadful state all this time——'

'What do you mean, all this time?' he lashed back at her. 'I came across him up in the bush three days ago and the vet's been away. He's due back now and his nurse tells me he'll be along here today for sure. If your brother——'

'Oh, don't start that again!' Jacqui was too over-wrought to choose her words. 'It's all your fault, the whole thing!' As she bent over to lift the horse's hoof, her flare of anger died away in concern, for the flesh around the hoof was painfully overgrown. 'Don't worry, old pal, you won't have to stay like this for much longer. Now that I'm here I'll look after you.' She swung around to eye Bradley Kent. 'Why,' she demanded, 'have you put him away up here by himself?'

He shrugged. 'You know the way other horses take to a new chum in the paddock. I reckoned he had enough to contend with as it is without that. He isn't exactly in a condition to take on fights right now.'

'I suppose,' she agreed reluctantly. Her gaze swept over the horse's matted coat, tangled with bidi-bids, the torn flesh, dried blood and long cuts. 'Now that I'm here I'll get going on treating those wounds of his. If you'll show me where you keep your disinfectants and the rest of it I'll get started right away.'

'You'd do better,' he advised in his maddening authori-tative way, 'to hang on till the vet gets here and go along with what he says.'

Jacqui ignored that, since she had no intention of taking his advice. She murmured, half to herself, 'I've had Pancho for five years and he's never looked like this.'

'England,' Bradley Kent observed in his offhanded tone, 'is a heck of a long way away.'

'Are you blaming me for going away and leaving him?' She hadn't known she could feel so angry with anyone. 'How can you! When *you're* the one who——'

'Who rescued him? Was that what you were going to say?'

'You wouldn't help anyone,' she muttered, 'let alone a helpless animal.' She patted Pancho's head. 'But I'm here now. I'll look after you, get you better in no time.'

'If you go by what the vet says.'

She faced him, anger glittering in her eyes. 'How can I trust you of all people? How do I know you've asked him to come here and see Pancho?'

His drawling voice had a cutting softness. 'You could try taking a look down the driveway. Here he comes now.'

She spun around, lips parted in suprise. It was true. A dust-smeared pick-up truck was sweeping around the curving pathway to come to a stop by the woolshed. Bradley Kent put two fingers to his lips and gave a piercing whistle, the driver of the truck gave an answering toot on the horn and presently a short, thickset man of middle age wearing a white overall, came striding over the grass towards them.

Brad tossed off introductions swiftly, carelessly. 'Gary, our local vet—Jacqui. It's her horse.'

He had a reassuring smile for Jacqui, but she saw his smile fade into a professional mask as his glance went to her mount. No wonder, she thought, for what must he think of any girl who had allowed her horse to get into this pitiable condition?

'I've been away in England,' she heard her own voice babbling an explanation. 'I left the horse with my brother Nick. Of course it wasn't his fault that Pancho got into this state, all these cuts and wounds and sores . . .' Why was she going on and on? Useless anyway, because at mention of Nick's name a shutter had come down over the vet's face. Of course, the disquieting thoughts flew through her mind, Bradley Kent had spread all these lies about Nick and of course everyone believed him. Why shouldn't they? It was only she who knew the truth of the matter, and even she couldn't refute it all, not with Nick away from here and not letting her know what had really happened. So she said no more as the vet ran his hands over the horse, closely inspecting the festering wounds and picking up each hoof in turn.

'No permanent harm done,' he gave his opinion, but he was looking at Bradley Kent and not at her. Bradley must have told him a good story, she thought bitterly. She wrenched her mind back to the present. 'I'll trim his hooves, that will make him feel a lot happier, and get some of the thorns out. A shot of penicillin first, though, to clear up the infection.'

Jacqui watched in silence as he completed his tasks. Through it all the vet addressed all his remarks to Bradley Kent, and that hurt. How utterly callous he must think her. She remembered girls she had known in the pony club at home who had treated their mounts as playthings, to be ridden or jumped at hunts and gymkhanas and left to their own devices for months at a time, to suffer injuries through barbed wire and neglect. And that was the sort of girl the vet thought her to be! She'd half a mind to argue the matter, to put it to him that Pancho's pitiable state was in no way due to her, that she had trusted her brother to care for the horse, but something untoward had happened. But how could she when she didn't know the circumstances herself? Besides, the way the vet was talking to Bradley, anyone could see that he regarded Bradley as someone whose opinion he respected. If he only knew!

'Right!' At long last the vet was speaking to her instead of Bradley. 'He'll take a lot of nursing back to health, feeding on the best of grass, cleaning and treating all the sores.' He packed away knife and syringe in his bag. 'I'll drop off the stuff you'll need for medication at the stables and after that it's up to you! I take it you'll carry on with the treatment. You're free to give some time to getting him right?'

'Oh yes!'

An approving smile lighted up the vet's rugged features and for the first time he looked *really* friendly, so friendly that Jacqui wondered if the usual expected reaction from newly met male acquaintances was working again. Or maybe her concern for her horse had got through to him. 'I only want to get him well again. I mean, I owe it to him——' On meeting the satirical glint in Bradley Kent's eyes she stopped short. 'In a way,' she added.

'That's okay, then. If you can fix him up yourself——'

'Oh, I will! I'll do anything——'

Anything? Suddenly she felt sick in her midriff. What had she promised? To stay on here on Bradley Kent's property, living goodness knows where. Not that living conditions mattered but being beholden to him was something else!

The vet unaware of the conflicting feelings raging within her, had turned towards Bradley. 'Any other problems you want me to sort out while I'm here, Brad?'

'You could take a look at a couple of the mares up on the hill,' Bradley told him, 'just a check-up.'

'Right!' As the two men began to walk away, Bradley tossed over his shoulder to Jacqui, 'Won't be long. Wait here and I'll pick you up on the way back to the house.'

She was only too pleased to be here with Pancho, even though it wrung her heart to see the coat she had brushed to silky smoothness was now long and matted. She began dragging bidi-bids and twigs from the long tail and mane. If only she had asked the vet to leave her a brush. All the time another more urgent matter, tugged at her mind. She didn't trust Bradley Kent to care for her horse. She knew all too well the type of man he was, and the idea of him or his staff spending their time tending Pancho was just something that couldn't possibly happen. Somehow then she must contrive to be around here for some weeks herself. It was the thought of asking him to put her up at his home that bothered her. It was something she couldn't do, she just couldn't! The words would stick in her throat, and anyway the attempt would be doomed to disaster. He had no time for her at all, and as to inviting her to stay on his property . . . After their stormy encounter last night, after Nick, after everything.

A little later, as she got into his car once again and they followed the vet's truck down to the stables, she still could think of no way out of her dilemma, there just wasn't any.

She put the problem from her mind as the vet took the necessary medication from his bag and told her how to apply it. She was so *aware* of Bradley waiting in the car, watching silently, and she just knew what he was thinking, that she didn't explain to the veterinary man that she already knew all the instructions he was giving her. Yes, she would attend to the wounds once a day, take off the bandage on Pancho's leg in a week's time. If she had any problems just give him a buzz and he'd be right out to check on the treatment and hurry up the healing. He made it all sound so simple.

'Come into the house,' Bradley invited as the vet climbed back into the truck. 'That's thirsty work you've been doing.'

'Sorry, not a hope. I've got a pile-up of work waiting. I'll be lucky if I get through half the calls by tonight. It's urgent cases only today. Sometimes I wonder if it's worth taking a week's holiday when you work twice as long hours afterwards to make up for it. Oh well, that's the way the cookie crumbles!'

Jacqui smiled a farewell. He didn't appear to be overworked, she thought. He looked cheerful and happy as if he enjoyed every minute of his occupation. Odd, his having made Pancho an urgent call today. Of course the horse desperately needed attention, but it seemed out of character for Bradley to have insisted on the visit. She told herself that no doubt for reasons of his own Bradley had bulldozed the vet, just as he did everyone else to suit his own purposes, into coming here today. He was like that—hadn't she proof of it in the way he had treated Nick? Just wait until she heard from Nick and she would be really able to hold her own in an argument with Bradley Kent.

Meantime she was anxious to attend to Pancho and she waited impatiently until Bradley returned to take the wheel. He made no move to start the motor, however, but raised a hand in farewell as the truck swept past them.

'So now you know,' came the deep vibrating tones.

'I know all right. Look, I'd like to start on that treatment right now. I know what to do——'

'Half an hour won't make all that much difference,' he told her in an impassive voice. 'I'll run you up to the house and you can freshen up first.'

That made some sense. 'All right, then.' Once again the habit of thinking her thoughts aloud tripped her up. Why hadn't she realised before that of course he would be a married man, and that made her position here even more hopeless. She said hesitantly, 'Your wife——'

He put a hand to the starter motor and they moved up the winding driveway. He flicked her a cool glance. 'What wife?'

'I just thought,' she was frantically searching for words to cover the slip, 'she might have wondered who I am and what I'm doing here.' She drew a deep breath and put out a feeler. 'The vet seemed to think that I should be——'

'Why would a wife make any difference?' Was he warning her off any personal involvement with him once again? Her cheeks burned hotly at the thought. 'We keep open house at Waiwhetu,' his impersonal tone was as dashing to her taut nerves as a douche of cold water. 'Strangers here are nothing out of the ordinary. There's always some bod turning up on the doorstep wanting shelter, for one reason or another.'

'Or another?' She couldn't resist the gibe.

He simply ignored her. 'We put out the welcome mat for them——'

'*All* of them?' She flung him a taunting glance.

'And send them on their way.'

Jacqui tapped a thumbnail on her teeth in a worried gesture. A reluctant hospitality, was that what he was offering her? One thing was for sure, she thought wryly, so far as he personally was concerned, for her the welcome mat definitely wasn't out!

CHAPTER THREE

Lost in her problems, Jacqui sat silent as they swept around a curve of the winding driveway. They passed a line of sheepdogs chained in their kennels and the wild barking of the working dogs followed them as they skirted the blue glimmer of a swimming pool. Soon they were drawing up on a wide concrete driveway of the rambling ranch-style home. Wicker chairs and table stood on the long open porch running along the front of the dwelling and curtains fluttered from open french doors.

Bradley came around the car to open the passenger door and together they moved up a short flight of steps and crossed the sun-splashed terrace.

'Come on in!' After a moment's hesitation Jacqui preceded him into a thickly carpeted foyer with its great Chinese vases set on stands and cascading with attractive floral arrangements. Through the tumult of her emotions the thought went through Jacqui's mind that even if Bradley had no wife, a woman lived here who cherished beautiful things.

The next moment he flung open the door leading off the wide hallway and she met the startled gaze of two women who were seated in the spacious lounge room.

'Brad! You're back!' A short stout woman of middle age with frizzy golden hair glanced from Brad to Jacqui enquiringly.

'Jacqui Masters, this is my aunt Tessa,' Brad tossed off the introduction briefly, 'and my cousin Bernice.'

With another part of her mind Jacqui found herself taking immediately to the dark girl, whose cropped dark hair and twinkling eyes lent her an elfin look. Or maybe she felt attracted to her because this was the first friendly glance she had had in days. Blame Bradley for that!

The older woman got to her feet, smiling a welcome. 'Sit down here, my dear.' She wore a lot of make-up, Jacqui noticed, and a cluster of gold chains hung around the neck of her immaculately tailored dress.

'Jacqui's come to see about her horse,' Brad explained offhandedly. 'Just as we got here, the vet showed up so we've got the treatment all sorted out. He'll be okay.' He didn't elaborate on how Jacqui's horse happened to be at his home, and both women were looking a little mystified.

Jacqui took a deep breath. I might as well let them know right away who I am, and get it over with, she thought. She said a little breathlessly, 'My brother Nick has—had the run-off down by the main road. He went away and Bradley took Pancho back to his place.' She waited for the expected reaction to Nick's name. Surprise, a stunned moment of silence, aversion? It didn't happen.

'That's nice,' Aunt Tessa murmured politely. 'I'm sure you'd like some tea after that trip on the dusty roads. I don't need to ask Bradley how he feels about that— Bernice,' she turned to her daughter, 'go and ask Mrs Beeson to bring in a tray, will you?'

'Would you excuse me?' Jacqui took the opportunity to follow the other girl out of the room.

'Don't tell me,' Bernice threw over her shoulder with a smile, 'you want the bathroom? It's three doors down the hall. Was it a long drive from the bush farm?' she asked with interest.

'About an hour.' Jacqui turned into a doorway, adding silently, and it felt like a lifetime! But what a relief to know that mention of Nick's name hadn't rung any bell to either the pixie-faced girl or her mother. Thank heaven for small mercies!

When she returned to the lounge room she stood for a moment unnoticed at the open doorway. She was struck anew by the luxury of her surroundings, the faded Persian carpets and exquisitely made furniture. Her gaze lifted to the family portraits hanging on the walls. Even in her swift appraisal she realised that one portrait, depicting a

man of Victorian times, bore a striking resemblance to
Bradley. The unmistakable air of pride and self-assurance,
the cool grey eyes and well-cut lips, and Bradley was
devastatingly good-looking too, though she hated to admit
it. Everything she had seen so far added up to wealth and
luxury and made her think all over again how unfair life
was. She hated being here in his house, accepting his
reluctant hospitality, yet at the moment it seemed that
she could do nothing about it.

'Here we are!' A pleasant-faced woman with short-cut
greying hair and a cheerful smile put down the tea-tray on a
low table. 'How are you, Brad?' And before he could answer,
'Did you come across anything up-country you fancied?'

Briefly his gaze flickered to Jacqui and, to her horror,
she felt the tell-tale colour creeping up her cheeks. 'Not
really. Mrs Beeson, this is Jacqui. Mrs Beeson's one we just
couldn't get along without.'

'It's my cooking that's the attraction!' Jacqui liked the
housekeeper at sight. There was something wholesome
and appealing about her clear tanned skin and friendly
smile. Clearly to Mrs Beeson Jacqui meant no more than
one more visitor to the house. Unconsciously she sighed.
If only it were the truth! Her gaze went to Bradley. Was
it because of their mutual antagonism that she couldn't
seem to stop her gaze straying towards him? He was smiling and at ease. Why not? He had everything his own
way, didn't he? Oh, he could be friendly enough on his
own terms, it seemed.

'What's been happening?' he was asking his aunt. He
had been out of touch for a day or two, so they would
have to fill him in on the latest news of the station. How
about Queenie, had she foaled?

'Not yet.' It was Bernice who answered.

'Don't worry,' his aunt told him laughingly. 'You
haven't been forgotten about while you've been away.
There's a pile of mail waiting to be opened in your office
and a list of folks wanting you to ring them—stock agents,
your lawyer in town, some top-dressing firm and half the

members of the hunt club. I'd say you're going to be kept busy for quite a while in the office.'

He groaned, 'Don't tell me! If there's one thing I loathe, it's office work.'

'Don't forget Sue,' Bernice put in. 'She's been ringing here every hour on the hour wanting to know when you'd be back.'

'Has she now?' It seemed to Jacqui that the strong lines of his deeply-tanned face softened. 'I'll give her a buzz.'

Bernice said, 'She said to tell you she'd be over here this afternoon anyway.'

'How about Rick?'

Bradley's teasing gaze was fixed on Bernice's face and under his look Jacqui saw a faint colour stain the girl's cheeks. 'How would I know?'

'He's down in the stockyards drafting steers, if you're looking for him. You know Rick, he never minds having an audience around, especially a feminine one,' said his aunt.

'That's the trouble,' Bernice said very low.

'And Chris?' Bradley's expression had sobered. 'Has he got back to work, by any chance?'

Bernice shook her head.

'In the shed painting, then?'

Bernice shook her head. 'Not that I know of. He stays in his room and we've scarcely seen him.'

In the silence Jacqui's gaze went from Bradley's face to Bernice.

'We've got a budding artist in the family.' Aunt Tessa turned to Jacqui. 'He likes to be on his own, but you can usually find him in the old shed at the back of the orchard. He's really quite talented.' Jacqui couldn't help wondering if the blonde woman with her tinkling gold chain necklaces and profusion of rings on plump fingers was really qualified to give an opinion on the matter.

'I don't think you've told Jacqui anything about the set-up here,' Aunt Tessa taxed Bradley. 'Three brothers,' she ran on, 'and all so different. Brad here runs the place, he's the manager, and Rick shares the work. Chris is the artistic one, he's not really interested in sheep farming, but——'

'We think—hope,' Bernice cut in, 'that he'll be famous one day and we'll all be ever so proud of him.' She added on a sigh, 'Once he gets over this setback he's had lately.'

'We don't live here as a rule,' Aunt Tessa gave a tinkling laugh, 'but Bradley's mother, my sister, was called away on a trip to England. She certainly deserved a break, looking after everyone all these years. I happened to be staying here at the time and I suggested, "Why not go and take your time? You haven't seen your daughter since she left New Zealand three years ago, and, now she's got the new baby. You can rely on me to hold the fort while you're away." After all, Mrs Beeson is an excellent housekeeper, I'm sure I'm not needed all that much.'

'Oh, but you are!' Bradley's twinkling eyes were on his small ebullient aunt. 'Those floral arrangements are really something!'

'And you take care of the entertaining,' Bernice put in. She confided to Jacqui, 'Coming here just worked in nicely for me too. I've just started school teaching and with six weeks' holiday—Wow! Besides, I like the country——'

'Just the country?' Brad's voice held a warm inflection that was new to her. He could be very different to any girl but her! She brought her mind back to Aunt Tessa. 'And where do you live, dear?' the older woman was enquiring idly.

'A long way from here—at least, that's where I used to live before I went away to England for a trip. My dad had a farm at Wanganui. He——'

'What did you say your name was?' Aunt Tessa was eyeing her with interest.

'Masters.'

'Now isn't that a coincidence! I thought the name rang a bell. Your mother's name was Helen Masters?'

'Yes, it was. Did you know her?'

'Know her! My dear, we shared an overseas trip together. It was a trip to Australia organised by the Women's Institute organisation for their members all over the country. Your mother and I shared hotel rooms, and the fun we had! I'll never forget that trip! I was so shocked to see in the papers just a few months later that she'd died. And to think,' she regarded Jacqui with a warm glance, 'that you're her daughter. Where are you staying, my dear? I hope it's somewhere handy.'

'I'm not, actually. I'm sort of in between. You see, I only got back to this country a few days ago.'

'Then you'll come to us and stay for as long as you please—it's no use——' she put up a plump beringed hand, 'I won't hear of your saying "no". You'll enjoy it. Such a change for you, and we'd love to have you. Bernice needs some company, another girl——'

'Not any old girl, Mum,' Bernice flashed her pixyish smile. 'You!'

'It's awfully kind of you to ask me.' Jacqui was uneasily aware of Bradley's watchful look. She could make a good guess at what he was thinking. Just an opportunist, like her brother. First she pushes herself into the cottage, now she's worming her way in here.

'Bradley——' Aunt Tessa's effusive tones appealed to the man standing at her side. He was listening, just listening, Jacqui thought distractedly. '*You* make her stay! Tell her we insist that she comes to us for as long as she likes.'

He said tersely, 'It's over to her.'

The thoughts flew wildly through Jacqui's mind. If it weren't for Pancho and those horrible injuries he'd suffered ... but she could cure those, given time. Could that be her own voice saying brightly, happily, 'If you're sure it won't put you out. Just until my horse gets well again.' She threw him a challenging look. Let Bradley think what he pleased of her, this was something she must do. He didn't want her in his home any more than she wanted to stay here, but he had already told her that he kept open house at Waiwhetu.

He said coolly, 'I'll get your bag,' and turned away.

How could the other two women not notice his off-putting expression, she wondered, or the ice that dripped in his tone? Maybe they had preferred to ignore it. All at once the tea she was sipping had no taste. Bradley seemed to make a habit of ruining her meals, she thought. Deep down, however, another thought intruded. She must forget about her own feelings and concentrate on getting Pancho back to health, after that she could please herself. But dear Lord, it could be a matter of weeks and weeks. How was she going to endure it?

A little later, as Bernice led her along the long carpeted corridor, Jacqui glanced towards the closed doors on either side. 'Goodness, are all these rooms bedrooms?'

Bernice smiled. 'Most of them. Bradley's office is opposite, though goodness knows how he ever finds the time to do any paper work. Here he comes now with a stock agent.'

Jacqui felt relieved that they were turning into a bedroom. She had had more than enough of Brad's cool-eyed stare for one day, and heaven only knew what he thought of her now.

Bernice, happily unaware of the conflict of emotion in the mind of her newly arrived guest, was saying happily, 'You're lucky, you're on the sunny side of the house!' She flung open a long window, letting in a view of the orchard. It was a delightful room, Jacqui thought. Even in her distraught state of mind she was aware of the lilac-coloured drapes, the soft pale green carpeting on the floor, delightful flower prints on the walls. 'There's swags of room for your gear.' Bernice flung open the wardrobe door.

'Thanks.' Jacqui spoke absently. Suddenly she had realised what she had let herself in for in coming here. She ran the tip of her tongue over dry lips.

'Don't look so worried.' Bernice flung herself down on the filmy white nylon bedcover. 'Mum's awful,' she ran on, 'she practically forces folk into staying here. It's just selfishness really, because she gets a bit bored. She's a town person really, and she misses her bridge club. You don't need to stay if you don't want to.'

'It's not that.' Did her tumult of mind show so much? 'I'd love to stay.' *Liar*. 'Was I looking worried?' she wondered. 'If I did, it's got nothing to do with anything here.' And that was another whopper. 'Truly.'

The twinkle in Bernice's dark eyes deepened. 'You don't need to tell me. It's boy-friend trouble, isn't it? Some man has let you down badly and you just can't think of anything else?'

Jacqui gave a rueful smile. 'In a way. But it's all a big mistake,' she added quickly. Once I find out what really happened——'

'Don't worry about him,' Bernice advised practically, 'he's probably not worth the worry anyway,' she sent Jacqui a laughing glance. 'Or is he?'

Into Jacqui's mind flashed a picture of Nick's smiling face. 'I think so.'

'Can't do anything about that, then. Tell me, how did Bradley happen to come across you? Mum and I only just arrived to stay with him ourselves, so everything's new to us too.'

'Oh, I was staying in the cottage on the run-off expecting to find my brother there. But there was some slip-up and he—wasn't there. I was just wondering how on earth I could get back to civilisation when Bradley turned up. He told me he had Pancho at his place and that the horse was in a pretty bad state with being on his own and all, and offered to bring me over to see him.'

Bernice nodded in agreement. 'That would be Bradley. He's like that.' Jacqui was relieved that the other girl had evinced no curiosity regarding the time element. She probably imagined that Bradley had turned up at the cottage this morning. She wrenched her mind back to the light tones. 'I knew there was something wrong with one of the horses here. Bradley's been phoning all around the district trying to get another vet to come out. He was really worried about your horse.'

'Bradley?' Jacqui was so astonished, she let the surprise show. 'Worried over Pancho?'

'You bet he was!'

'But why should he——'

'Gosh, he looks after everyone on the place, and that goes for the stock too. You don't know him very well, do you?'

You'd be surprised if you knew how well I know him—but Jacqui made the observation silently.

'You know something?' Bernice's gaze had gone to the air sticker on Jacqui's travel bag. 'You might have just arrived from London, but anyone could tell you're a Kiwi girl. It's the accent that gives you away.'

'Really?' Jacqui was feeling so relieved at the other girl's change of subject that she launched into a spirited account of her flatlife in London. 'Look,' she zipped open her travel bag and shook out a cream silky blouse. 'How do you like this? You can have it if you like, it's about your size.'

'Super!' Bernice slipped on the garment and eyed her reflection in the mirror with approval.

After Bernice had left her the full enormity of what she had done hit her once again, but she wasn't going to back out now. Bradley would just have to put up with having her around the place. And after all, there was no need for them to see much of each other. She argued away a niggling feeling of guilt by telling herself that because of Nick, Bradley owed her something, a whole lot more than a few weeks' lodging. If Nick were here he would agree with her.

Meantime, she had no intention of wasting precious time in unpacking her belongings when she could be getting on with the job for which she was here. Swiftly she changed into shabby jeans and a worn cotton top, then she hurried out of the front door. The distance to the stables that had seemed such a short distance in Bradley's car now seemed to be endless, but at last she reached the big open sheds that had once housed carriages and sulkies in an earlier era.

As she collected the various medications she needed, she mused that whatever his shortcomings, Bradley kept a good stock of veterinary supplies. She piled jars and bottles into the air travel bag she had provided herself with and threw in the parcel left by the vet. Then she filled a plastic bucket with water, threw towels over her shoulder, and plodded up the winding path leading to the hill paddock above. When she opened the gate the horse caught sight of her and once again came limping towards her. The sight of his thin frame wrung her heart, but she forced herself to concentrate on getting him back to health and made a start by cleaning the open wounds on his side and applying a dusting of powder and healing ointment.

Absorbed in her task as she was, the hours flew by without her noticing. Once, alerted by the sound of hoof-beats on the path, she glanced up to see two riders approaching the paddock, Bernice and the young man whom she had seen in the stockyards on her arrival. A few moments later Bernice dismounted and hurried towards Bernice. 'Hi! Seeing you missed out at lunchtime, these are for you. Catch!'

Jacqui caught the paper bag and peered inside. 'Peaches *and* apples from the orchard! Thanks!'

Already, however, Bernice was turning away. She looked happy and animated as she waved a hand to Bernice. 'See you later!' Soon the riders vanished over the rise.

It was some time later, when she was brushing Pancho's tangled mane, that Bradley's car swept up to the gate of the paddock and Jacqui looked up to see him approaching across the grass. With him was a girl, blonde, tall, thirtyish and by far the most beautiful—there was no other word to describe her—girl she had ever seen. The two came to a stop at the gate and the tall girl wearing jodhpurs, her feet planted far apart, regarded Jacqui disapprovingly.

'Good grief!' It came as something of a shock to Jacqui that this lovely girl spoke in a voice that was deep and forceful and downright bossy. Sue! It must be Sue!

'I've seen some pretty rotten ways to treat a horse,' she was saying, eyeing Jacqui accusingly, 'but this beats the lot! What in heaven's name have you done to him?'

Jacqui opened her lips to speak, then closed them again.

The temptation to angrily deny the charge was hard to resist, but she knew if she spoke at all she would lose her temper—again—and how that would please Bradley! She tightened her soft lips and brushed back her hair that was falling over her dust-smeared cheek. All at once she was conscious of her shirt, stained with smears of yellow disinfectant, her grimy hands. Her glance went to Bradley, but she might have known that he would be no help to her at all.

'Jacqui's here to do something about it,' he observed carelessly. 'Let's let her get on with it, shall we?' His cool glance flickered over her. 'You've got everything you want for the job?'

'Yes, *thank* you!' She spat the words at him.

'She's got her work cut out, it will take weeks to put him right—teach her a lesson, maybe,' Sue said to Bradley as they turned away.

Jacqui resisted an impulse to hurl the horse-brush in the direction of all that perfection. Was it her undeniable beauty that gave Sue the idea that she knew everything, could tell everyone else what they should do? Oh, they were two of a kind, Sue and Bradley! So that was the type of woman Bradley preferred. A woman in her early thirties, self-assured and dominating, if the episode just now were anything to go by. The odd thing was that she had a vague feeling of having seen the blonde woman somewhere before today, but how could one ever have forgotten beauty like that? She must be mistaken.

She brushed the horse's coat vigorously, her angry thoughts keeping time with the strokes. Oh, she was hateful! Hateful! And so was he! At that moment the piercingly strong feminine tones reached her on the clear air. 'Girls like her shouldn't be allowed to keep a horse. If I had my way——' Jacqui's hand stilled and she gazed, tight-lipped, at the tall girl who was sliding into Bradley's car.

The afternoon slipped away and the sun was low in the sky when at least Jacqui gathered together the assortment of ointments and bottles, brushes and bandages. At least she knew that Pancho was more comfortable than he had

been for many weeks, and with all this clean good grass
... 'That's it for today, mate. I'll be back to see you
tomorrow——'

'Can I help you carry all that?' She swung around to
meet the gaze of a tall, thin youth with a singularly sweet
smile.

'That would be a help, if you would.' They went
through the gate and he fastened it behind them.

Jacqui said with a smile, 'You're Chris?'

'That's right.' A shadow passed over the pale face.
'They told you about me?'

She didn't know how to reply. 'Told me? No, why
should they?'

A sulky expression crossed his face. 'They're always on
about it, up at the house. Just because,' he hesitated, 'well,
I've had a bit of a blow and it sort of knocked me.'

He did appear like someone who had been ill, she
thought, taking in the dark shadows under his eyes. To
change the subject she said cheerfully, 'Well, I've only
just arrived here today, so I don't know anything about
anyone. The only sick thing I know of is my horse that
you saw back in the paddock, and he's going to be fit
again now that I'm here to look after him.'

'I don't get it.' He turned towards her his apathetic
gaze. 'Brad said he brought the horse back from the
bush farm. He was in a terrible state when he found him—
just about starved to death!'

Jacqui felt a pang of guilt. If only they wouldn't keep
on in this strain. The words made her feel more at fault
than ever, and it wasn't even the truth!

'That guy up there—' Chris choked, and fell silent.

'I know, my brother Nick. He was looking after Pancho
while I was away in England——'

'Him?' She stared at him in surprise, for the apathetic
eyes were now ablaze with emotion, his mouth working
pitiably. 'Nick Masters? You're *his* sister?'

'That right.' She eyed him in bewilderment. 'Why,
what's wrong?'

'You can ask *me* that? What's wrong?' Was it her imagination that made his thin face seem even paler than before? 'I'm going on!' he said abruptly, and hurrying ahead down the path, he left her to follow.

Well! Jacqui went on down the dusty track. The youth seemed to be in a pitiable state of mind, a victim of his jangled nerves. What could she have said to upset him? Something about Nick?'

More affected by the incident than she cared to admit, even to herself, she went on thoughtfully to the stable where she busied herself in putting away the horse medicines and ointments in their box. Whatever scruples she had felt in agreeing to stay here were now intensified by her meeting with the overwrought younger brother—and she was to face him at the evening meal tonight.

That evening when Jacqui went into the lounge room, a swift glance told her that neither Bradley nor his young brother Chris were there. Aunt Tessa, her plump fingers busy with the crochet work that never seemed far from her hands, sent her a friendly smile. Bernice, who was seated on the floor, hands crossed around her knees, was leaning against a young man who was idly strumming a guitar. 'Two more men you haven't met, Jacqui,' she said laughingly. 'The tough-looking one is Bill Lewis——'

'Head shepherd to you.' A thick-set man with honest eyes and a friendly smile took her hand in an iron grip.

'And Rick——'

The young dark-haired man got to his feet, blue eyes in a lean tanned face flickering over Jacqui with obvious appreciation. He wasn't so tall as his brother Bradley, the thoughts flew through Jacqui's mind, nor did he possess Bradley's undeniable charisma, but he appeared happy and relaxed and infinitely more approachable.

'So this,' he grinned, 'is the girl with a horse in need of nursing care?'

She was so grateful to him for not censuring her on animal cruelty that she flashed him a warm smile. 'That's me!'

'He sure needs some attention, but a pretty girl can

work miracles,' white teeth flashed in a mahogany-tan face, 'and that nag is surely in need of a miracle!'

From a corner of her eye Jacqui was aware of Bernice's downcast expression. She's really in love with him, the thought came unbidden. Oh well, she has no cause to be jealous on my account. I'm not enamoured of either of Bradley's brothers, or him either, if it comes to that!

'You're fresh out from England, they tell me? I could have guessed that myself. You don't see that sort of complexion out here.'

Jacqui laughed. 'It's only temporary, all this pink and white. Give me a few weeks back here in a New Zealand summer——'

'Here's Bradley,' said Aunt Tessa suddenly. Jacqui too had caught the sound of masculine footsteps approaching the outside washroom. 'That means we won't have to wait dinner tonight! You never can tell what hour of the night the men will come in from their work.'

Jacqui scarcely caught the words. She was wondering if the two men she had just met knew who she *really* was. Bradley's slanderous assessment of Nick's character one would imagine to be enough to cause them to dislike her on sight, yet they had shown no particular reaction to her name. All at once she had to know.

'I wonder if you came across my brother Nick,' she said in her soft throaty tones. 'He had the bush farm down by the main road.'

'Is that right?' Bill's tone was cheerfully unconcerned. 'I heard there was a guy over there for a while, but Bradley said he'd given away the idea of farming, only stuck it out for a few months.'

'I gave him a lift to town one day when his car broke down,' Rick said carelessly. 'He had a girl with him, a real looker!'

'That would be Nick!' Jacqui laughed more in relief than in amusement. Clearly the two men knew no more about Nick's life on the bush farm than she herself, less indeed, and best of all, Bradley hadn't let them in on his fabrications about unpaid debts and unfulfilled promises. That story, it seemed, he kept only for her. Obviously they were ignorant of any connection between Nick and Chris's breakdown in health.

The next moment she became aware that Bradley had entered the room. Could it be her imagination that made her feel he brought with him an air of electric excitement? He had changed from working gear into a fawn open-necked shirt and brown corduroy slacks and his dark hair was still damp from the shower.

'Hi, folks!' He crossed the room and moving to the cocktail cabinet, began to pour drinks. 'Jacqui?' She met his enquiring look with a defiant glance. She had wondered how he would greet her tonight, but if he were feeling a deep reluctance to having her here, his closed expression gave nothing away.

'A small sherry for me, please.'

'Right!' His tone was as impersonal as ever. He tossed a smile towards his aunt and Bernice. 'I know your preferences,' he said, and soon he was handing around the drinks.

'Men always seem to have so much to talk about in the country,' Aunt Tessa murmured to Jacqui, her gaze on the masculine group gathered around the cocktail cabinet. 'All those sheep and cattle and Rugby and the possums and the weather, there's just no end to it. Bradley's a real man's man, if you know what I mean, but still, I would have thought that tonight, with a girl like you here, he might show a bit of interest. I mean to say, someone who looks so young and appealing and who doesn't happen to be a cousin, like Bernice, although really she's an adopted daughter and no relation to Bradley or his brothers——'

'Thank goodness!' Bernice said with a laugh.

'But of course there's Sue,' Aunt Tessa jabbed the crochet hook angrily into the yarn, 'unfortunately! Looks aren't everything, not when she's so bossy and arrogant and not at all the type of girl my sister wants as Bradley's wife. But of course he'll go his own way when it comes to choosing a mistress for Waiwhetu. If only ...' she broke off on a sigh, her gaze resting on Jacqui's young face.

Jacqui could scarcely explain to this friendly match-maker that the last thing in the world she wanted was for the boss to show the slightest interest in her, especially in *that* particular way! She hated him in a way she had never hated anyone in her whole life, so why, the thought came unbidden, was she feeling curious about his love life?

Sue couldn't stay to dinner or you'd have met her,' Bernice was saying. 'Her folk run a sheep station some miles away, they're our nearest neighbours as neighbours go up here in the outback. She rides over most days to see Bradley. She's the most gorgeous thing you ever saw.' Bernice's tone was untinged with envy and Jacqui wondered would the other girl had felt differently had Rick been the object of the frequent visits. But why did Sue always come to Bradley? Why didn't he go to see her? And what did it matter to her anyway? Aloud she said, I did see Sue today when I was up in the paddock.' No need to go into the humiliating details of their meeting. 'Funny, I had the feeling all the time that I'd seen her before somewhere, but of course it's impossible.'

'Not really,' said Bernice. 'Remember the tall blonde girl in jodhpurs riding a horse over green paddocks in the sunshine that was a TV commercial for New Zealand butter a year or two ago?'

'Of course! That girl was Sue——'

'Who else?' Bernice said laughingly, 'A champion show-jumper, and district beauty queen contest winner. What more could a girl want?'

Only Bradley! Now where on earth, Jacqui asked herself, had that ridiculous thought come from?

They were moving towards the dinner table when the housekeeper came into the room to speak to Aunt Tessa. 'A message from Chris, he said to tell you he won't be in to dinner. He's not feeling very well tonight, said he'd give the meal a miss.'

'Oh dear!' Aunt Tessa's beautifully made-up face had a

worried look. 'I do hope he's all right. Maybe I'd better go and see him.'

Bradley, who had overheard the message, said quietly, 'Leave him alone. He'll be okay! He's bound to have a few setback before he gets back on the right road.'

A little later, in spite of a niggling feeling of guilt concerning Chris, Jacqui found that she was enjoying the meal. The food was delicious, succulent slices of lamb served with home-grown peas and fresh beans, and slices of the sweet little pumpkins known as butternuts. The dessert that followed was made from stewed tamarillos, the tangy crimson oval-shaped fruit, with a fluffy meringue topping. Maybe, she mused, her enjoyment of the meal had a lot to do with Bernice, seated next to her, and Aunt Tessa's smiling face opposite her. They really wanted her here, and if she took care not to let her glance stray towards Bradley . . . Tonight, seated at the head of the table, he appeared very much the master of this vast station, the man in command who everyone here appeared to defer to—except herself.

When the meal was finished, the men moved away to the room with its pool table, leaving the womenfolk in the lounge room to chat desultorily as the characters of *Coronation Street* flashed on to the television screen.

'I suppose that this programme is light years behind the one showing in England right now?' Bernice prompted smilingly.

'I guess so,' Jacqui agreed, 'but it doesn't bother me any. I'm not a regular enough watcher to notice the difference in T.V. programmes.' The evening slipped away until Aunt Tessa laid down her lacy pink crochetwork and put up a hand to smother a yawn. 'I'm for bed. Are you girls staying up?'

'Not me,' Bernice rose to her feet, stretching her arms above her head. Her glance went to the hallway and Jacqui had an impression that Bernice had waited in vain for Rick to leave the pool room.

'Nor me,' said Jacqui.

''Night, you two.'

When the older woman had left the room, Jacqui's curiosity got the better of her and she couldn't resist putting a query to Bernice. 'I met Chris up in the paddock today. He doesn't look very well.'

'He's not,' Bernice agreed. 'You'd never take him for Bradley and Rick's brother, would you, he's so thin and weak-looking. He's twenty-one really, but he looks about seventeen. He never was strong, and after what happened last winter——'

'He told me he'd taken a knock. Did he mean—had he met with an accident or something?'

Bernice's elfin face sobered. 'No, nothing like that. He met a girl in Rotorua and he really fell hard for her, couldn't eat or sleep for thinking of her. I never met her, it was one of those whirlwind affairs and they got engaged two months after they first met.'

'What happened?'

Bernice shrugged her shoulders. 'She got friendly with someone else, a man in Rotorua. I don't know who he was. I think Bradley knows, but he never says anything. It wouldn't have been so bad if only Chris hadn't been such a weak sort of guy, physically I mean, but he just couldn't take it. He had a nervous breakdown, and after all these weeks, he's just starting to come right. He really took it hard, the girl breaking things off with him and taking up with another man. Of course he's always been rather delicate. He's a nice lad, thoughtful and kind of sweet. I only wish,' she said on a sigh, 'that it hadn't happened to him.'

You don't wish it any more than I do, Jacqui told herself with feeling. The story she had just learned explained a lot of things. It was Nick, with his easy charm, who had caused Chris's heartache and breakdown in health, and Bradley knew it! Now she understood the reason for his bitter, abrasive attitude towards her To have his brother humiliated and heartbroken because of Nick—how Bradley must have hated her brother for that!

CHAPTER FOUR

LEFT alone, Jacqui was about to follow the other two women when she was struck by a sudden thought. Pancho. She had an uneasy suspicion that she might have wound the bandage around his leg too tightly. At any rate, it would do no harm for her to take a walk up to the paddock and check. A glance through curtains she parted at the window showed her dark clouds scudding over the moon and tall trees swaying in the wind. In her bedroom she picked up her flashlight and made her way down the carpeted hall. The echo of masculine voices reached her from the pool room, but she met no one as she made her way out to the verandah.

Outside, drifting clouds obscured the moon and a soft rain was falling, but no matter. She hurried down the steps, opened the small gate and presently she was making her way towards the path winding up the slope. It was more difficult than she had anticipated to push against the strong wind as she went up the rutted track, but at last she gained the paddock where the dark blur of a horse was evident by the fenceline.

Oh *no*! For as she reached the horse she could see that his hoof was entangled in the wire. She made an effort to pull him free, for already his struggles had resulted in a jagged tear in the flesh. 'Oh, Pancho, how *could* you be so stupid!' At that moment, as if at a prearranged signal, the skies opened and rain slashed across her face and beat down on her head and shoulders. She made no effort to escape the downpour, her attention centred on the trapped animal. It took quite a time, but at last she managed to get him free of the wire. With luck, he shouldn't come to any further harm before morning. She watched him limp towards the shelter of a clump of tall trees, and only then did she realise that she was soaked to the skin.

She was moving towards the gate, head bent against the driving rain, when she collided with someone in the darkness. A beam of light shot across the drenched grass and she felt strong arms around her. 'Steady on! Where do you think you're going?'

'Brad!' She dashed the streaming water from her eyes and pushed dripping hair back from her face. 'What are you doing up here?'

'What do you think?' he demanded in a harsh tone. 'Keeping an eye on you! If you haven't got the sense to take a coat with you——' He had pulled off his wind-breaker and was flinging it around her shoulders.

'I don't *want* it!' She wriggled free.

'Well, you're going to have it, whether you want it or not!'

'I'm all right,' she said huffily. All at once she was unaccountably shivering. 'L-leave me alone!'

For answer, from behind her strong determined hands pulled the garment once more around her shoulders, his fingers digging into her flesh. 'Now will you do as you're told?'

She made an ineffectual effort to free herself from his grasp, but his hands were pinning her. 'Why should I?'

'Because you're asking for a dose of pneumonia if you don't!'

'You'd hate that, wouldn't you,' she said through chattering teeth, 'being lumbered with me as well as Pancho, to look after!'

He ignored her taunt. 'Hell, girl, didn't you see the storm coming?'

'It wasn't so bad when I came out.'

'Come *on*!' His disturbing touch dropped away as he marched her down the muddy track. It was easier to wear the garment herself, she decided, rather than to argue the matter further. Through the driving rain she glanced up to catch a glimpse of his set face, his dark hair plastered wetly across his forehead. 'What about you? You'll be soaked!'

He laughed, a deep masculine chuckle that was oddly attractive. 'It wouldn't be the first time. You should know that, you're a country girl.' All at once his tone hardened. 'You and Nick were brought up on a farm, or so you told me?'

'It's true.' She knew by the coldness in his voice that the mention of Nick's name had brought back his feelings of antagonism towards her brother and herself. The thought made her say crossly, 'You didn't need to follow me up here.'

'*Follow you!*' Too late she realised she had made a dreadful blunder. 'I was further up the hill, taking a look at one of my mares, she's due to foal any time now, when I realised there was someone down the slope. No one but you would be out in this weather without a coat, or a light——'

'I had a flashlight,' Jacqui protested with spirit, 'but it went out.'

'What were you doing up here anyway?'

'The same as you,' she cried triumphantly, 'checking my horse. And I'm glad I did, because he happened to be in big trouble. He'd caught his hoof in the fence wire and couldn't move. Goodness knows how badly cut about he'd have been by morning if I hadn't come along to free him. You know what wire can do to a horse!'

'I know.' The words were drowned by rolls of thunder that reverberated over the hills.

At that moment Jacqui stumbled and lost her balance. Those wretched tree roots in the path, she thought, as she felt her feet slip from under her. Just in time she was hauled to her feet by strong arms. The trouble was, she was feeling so very much *aware* of Brad's arm thrown around her shoulder to steady her. 'I'm all right now,' she said, and hoped he would put the breathless catch in her voice down to the weather conditions.

He took not the slightest notice of her words. Could it

be the rain and chill that was causing her to tremble so?
she wondered confusedly. For wasn't this the very even-
tuality she must guard against? For somewhere deep
down, way beyond common sense and important things
like his treatment of her and her hatred of him, she knew
that that way danger lay. If only he weren't aware of the
tumultuous state of her runaway emotions! She couldn't
trust herself to speak through the pulsing of her feelings.
How could a man's touch do these things to her? A
stranger, a man she couldn't stand at any price? It wasn't
fair! If it had been someone she liked a little, any other
man in the world—but it wasn't. This was Brad, her
enemy, who was practically dragging her along the path,
his arm thrown firmly around her in a way that brooked
no chance of a second slip on the unfamiliar track.

At last she gathered her thoughts together, for whatever
her feelings, there were things that must be said, important things. 'I hope it won't put you out,' she said breathlessly, 'my staying on for a time here at your aunt's invitation?'

'I thought we got that all sorted out before,' he said
curtly.

Stubbornly she persevered. 'I know, I know, but I had
no idea then that I'd have to stay for more than a few
days.'

'Forget it.' His tone was brusque. 'Like I said, we have
all sorts who put up here. Campers caught in summer
storms with their tents washed out, hunters who've run
out of supplies, stock agents on the way from here to there,
even the odd T.V. camera team filming a country commercial out in the backblocks.'

'How about waifs and strays?' She couldn't resist the
gibe.

At that moment a shaft of lightning played around them
and in that unguarded instant she caught an odd expression on his face, the reluctant twitch of his lips. But he
only replied, deadpan, 'All the time.'

It was no use, she couldn't crack that cool composure of

his. Clearly he included her in the category of a stranger to the district. Whether good or bad, male or female, it made no difference, all were assured of bed and board in his homestead. What had she expected, for heaven's sake, a welcoming committee?

'It's only because of Pancho.' She was forced to hurry along to keep pace with his long strides. She tried not to think about the masculine arm clasped so determinedly around her shoulders. 'His being in the vet's care and all that. Once my horse is all right again, I'll be off, and him too——' She broke off, struck by a horrifying thought. 'I keep saying *my* horse.' An incurable habit of honesty made her add slowly, 'I know you think of Pancho as part payment of a debt——'

'That's right.'

Oh, she might have known she could expect no quarter from him! She jerked herself free of his detaining arm and flung around to face him, uncaring of the rain pouring down. 'You can't mean you're going to keep him? You wouldn't! Even you couldn't be that low!'

'We'll discuss it later, shall we?' Roughly he clasped her hand in his and half pulled her along with him through the small gate and up the verandah steps.

Inside the house seemed deserted—luckily, Jacqui thought, for she had no wish to meet anyone, not in this sorry state. As she ran along the carpeted passage ahead of Brad, his voice reached her. He sounded as authoritative as ever. 'You'd better take a hot shower!'

'You don't need to tell *me* what to do!' she flung over her shoulder. She shot into her room and slammed the door behind her.

A few minutes later, however, conscious of shivering limbs and chattering teeth, she changed her mind. So long as he didn't know that she was taking his advice . . . First making certain that his door at the end of the passage was closed, she took pyjamas and a floral wrap and slipped into the bathroom. Luck was with her, for when, a little later, she emerged warm and glowing from a hot shower, the passage was deserted and she gained the sanctuary of her room without a further meeting with the boss.

In the morning Jacqui awakened to the melancholy lowing of cattle in the yards and it took her a few moments to realise where she was. Then as the events of the last few days flooded back to mind, she lay still, hands crossed behind her head, thinking. So Nick was the cause of Chris having had to part with the girl he loved so deeply. At last she understood the real reason for Brad's antagonistic attitude towards Nick, and herself. Not that Brad needed any further fuel for his smouldering anger towards her and her brother.

Something else niggled at the back of her mind, and at last she pinned it down. The New Year greeting card she had posted to Nick from London and found in his cottage on her arrival. Brad had told her that Nick had only been gone from Te Kainga two weeks earlier and that meant, she pursued the matter to its conclusion, that he had known of her expected arrival, but he hadn't let her know of his change of plan. But of course, something had happened to cause him to forget all about her. But surely he could have cabled her telling her not to come to join him? She thrust the traitorous thought aside. Nick would explain everything when he got in touch with her. Maybe he had left a forwarding address for her with their family lawyer in town. Why hadn't she thought of that before? Directly after breakfast she would ring through to the city and find out.

The meal proved to be an informal affair where everyone helped themselves to cornflakes and muesli, coffee and toast. As Jacqui had expected, the men had eaten breakfast at daybreak. A glance through the window showed her that Brad and one of the stockmen were ear-tagging steers penned in the yards. She recognised Brad's tall figure that was almost obscured in clouds of dust.

Aunt Tessa, immaculately attired in a tailored grey slack suit, came into the room with Jacqui. The frizzy golden hair evidently refused to be tamed into neat waves, but her make-up was carefully applied and gold chains still tinkled around her neck.

Bernice joined them a minute or so later. The small dark girl wore high-heeled wedge sandals and a cool green and white striped dress. She also, Jacqui noticed, was wearing a radiant smile.

'Rick's taking a day off today,' she said lightly to Jacqui. She helped herself to cornflakes. 'He's just getting himself spruced up, then he's taking me into Rotorua for a spin.'

Aunt Tessa was buttering a slice of toast. 'Why not,' she suggested brightly, 'take Jacqui along with you for the ride?'

'Oh no,' Jacqui protested quickly. 'I'm on duty here today with Pancho, remember? But thanks all the same.' She saw Bernice's tense features relax at her words.

A few minutes later a car drew up below the steps and Bernice jumped up from the table, her face radiant. 'See you later, folks. We'll be back some time!' She hurried away.

'I can't understand her,' said Aunt Tessa on a puzzled note. 'All those men she knows in town, there's one in particular, a young teacher she knows, who's always around at the house. He just won't take "no" for an answer, but Bernice wouldn't dream of taking his marriage proposals seriously. She doesn't bother with any of them, it's always Rick. Oh, she'll go out with other men, but in the end she gets tired of them. She's simply crazy about him, and if you ask me, he likes her well enough, in a cousinly sort of way, if you know what I mean.' Aunt Tessa didn't wait for an answer but ran on, 'I keep reminding him, and so does she, that she's only an adopted cousin, but it doesn't seem to do much good.'

She sighed and twisted the gold chains around her throat in a worried gesture. If only she would find someone else! Would you believe, she's known Rick since she was a child and it doesn't make a scrap of difference. With her, there's just no one to compare with him. Oh, there have been times when she knows he's been taking other girls out, and getting serious with one or two of them too. Those are the times when she takes up with someone else and really tries to put him out of her life, but it seems as though nothing really makes any difference. His flirtations come to an end after a while and back she comes, grabbing any excuse to stay at Waiwhetu, always hoping and hoping.' She paused to look at Jacqui thoughtfully. 'I wonder if you——'

Jacqui smiled. 'Sorry, it's no use asking me to try to influence her one way or the other. Even if I did try she wouldn't listen——'

'No,' Aunt Tessa agreed moodily, 'that's the worst of love. You can never do a thing about it, except watch and pray and hope things will somehow, some day, turn out for the best. That's the worst of only having one child,' she confided, 'you always want the best for them.'

Jacqui searched her mind for words. 'Maybe Rick likes her too.'

'Oh, he does! He does!' Aunt Tessa put down her coffee cup with a clatter. 'Trouble is he likes all his other girl-friends too, and they,' she added darkly, 'don't happen to be his cousins, or near enough.' After a moment she mused aloud, 'If only she didn't always let him know how crazy she is about him! You've only got to take one look at her face when she's going out with Rick to see how she feels.'

Jacqui didn't answer. She was wondering how if a girl cared, *really* cared deep down for a man, she could conceal her feelings. As she had never found herself in that state of mind, it was difficult to imagine. Maybe that wild madness they called love didn't really exist except in romantic stories and films. At that moment, out of no-where, a masculine face flashed on the screen of her mind: Brad's sensitive lips and brilliant grey eyes with a mocking glint. Swiftly she thrust the picture aside and said quickly. 'Is it all right if I phone someone in town?'

'Of course, my dear. Help yourself.'

The telephone was in the hall and as she dialled the

Auckland number Jacqui had a swift recollection of the
lawyer's old-fashioned office with its high ceiling and dark,
heavy furniture, the huge desk and everywhere, on floor
and desk and shelves, files and papers. 'Is that you, Mr
Gear? It's Jacqui Masters, remember?'

'Of course I remember. Glad to know you're back in
this country again. What can I do for you?'

'It's just about Nick,' she had rehearsed the query so
many times in her mind. 'I've just missed seeing him here
at Rotorua. He's left for overseas, I've been told, and I
wondered if he'd left any letter for me, or a message of
any sort, or money that was owing to me. I just thought
he might have contacted you.'

'Sorry, my dear,' he sounded genuinely regretful, 'but
we haven't had any dealings with Nick for almost a year,
but if anything turns up I'll let you know at once. Your
present address is——?'

She gave the Waiwhetu address. 'You will let me know
if you hear from Nick?'

'Certainly.'

'Thank you.' Jacqui replaced the receiver and turned
to find Brad standing at her side. He looked hot and dusty,
his forehead sheened with sweat, and she just knew that
those perceptive grey eyes hadn't missed the disappointment that shadowed her face. If only he would go away,
she thought irritatedly, but he seemed determined to make
the most of his victory over her. There was nothing for it
but to admit defeat.

'That was my lawyer—Nick's and mine,' she amended
briefly, 'if you must know.'

He said with deceptive mildness, 'I'm only waiting to
use the phone, that is, if you're through?'

'Oh yes, I'm through.'

'You didn't get any satisfaction, I take it, about your
brother,' the satirical curve of his lips deepened, 'or the
money you were going to collect?'

'No, I didn't!' To her horror she felt her bottom lip
beginning to tremble. Why must he commit to mind

every single word she said to him at a time when she had been filled with hope and confidence? Right now . . . a chill of doubt seemed to pass through her, but she pushed it aside. 'Just a moment, while I ring through to find out the cost of the toll call——'

'Forget it!'

But already her finger was dialling the numbers, and a few moments later she handed the receiver to Brad. 'It's all yours!' With heightened colour, she fled. It was a relief to escape at last from his disconcerting gaze.

A little later she went out into the clear bright sunshine. The summer storm of last night had passed and everywhere, bushes and leaves glistened and shone. In the long borders of the garden, the folded petals of red rosebuds were beaded with raindrops, and as she made her way up the damp track to the hill paddock above, the wind blew fresh and warm on her face, the sky was a tender blue.

The hours went swiftly by as she tended Pancho. As if he didn't have enough infections and cuts and slashes already, she told herself wryly, without the addition of a further cut during the night. Today, however, he looked better. He was eating the fresh green grass and when he moved, his limp wasn't so pronounced. After treating the infections and rebandaging the horse's leg, Jacqui brushed the long matted hair and trimmed away the knots.

That afternoon she wandered outside once again. Up till now she hadn't seen a great deal of her surroundings, she hadn't even seen the orchard. Now her steps took her through a back porch where the walls were hung with windbreakers and whips, sunhats and Maori kilts woven from flax. She went down some steps, passing a grassy enclosure evidently used for polo practice. A short distance away, a stocky-looking man with a grizzled head was weeding a huge expanse of vegetable garden. Jacqui answered his cheerful wave with a smile and opened a small gate leading into the orchard. There were peach trees, their branches drooping with the weight of great golden peaches, scarlet-flushed nectarines, and purple plums. Jacqui stood on tiptoe to select a peach of melting ripeness and bit into the soft flesh as she followed a narrow path winding among the fruit trees. Bunches of grapes, not yet ripe, festooned low fences and great trails of kiwi-fruit vines covered a nearby shed. The shed? Wasn't that the place where she had been told that Chris painted his pictures? She made her way towards the rough timber shack and peered in at the opening. Chris was lying on a low couch, his dull eyes scarcely changing their expression at the sight of her.

'Hi, Chris! May I come in?'

'If you like.' He raised himself to a sitting position, dropping his head in pale hands. 'I can't stop you, can I?'

It wasn't exactly an auspicious beginning to the visit, but she knew there was good reason for his lack of interest, especially where she was concerned. Oh well, she could only try to make him understand.

She moved into the shadowy room, blinking her eyes after the hot sunshine outside. All at once her glance went to a half-finished picture standing on the easel and her interest quickened. She took a step nearer to the canvas, her gaze taking in a picture of soaring bush-clad hills and, in the distance, a glimmer of waters of a blue lake.

'I know where that is,' her voice rang with excitement. 'This is the view you get from the bush farm at Te Kainga! I'd recognise those hills anywhere!'

For a moment a spark of interest flickered in his eyes. 'That's right.'

The next moment Jacqui regretted the impulsive words that would have brought his thoughts back to the bush farm, and Nick. 'Look,' she dropped to his side, 'I know how you feel about Nick and your girl-friend—*please*,' she begged, as his lips tightened, 'just listen to me for a moment! What you don't seem to realise is that all that has nothing to do with me. I only arrived back in this country a few days ago. I haven't set eyes on my brother for two years!'

She could almost see the thoughts passing through his

mind. At last he seemed to come to some decision. 'That's right,' he said slowly, 'you didn't know.'

'How could I? So let's forget about all that, shall we?' She tried out her warmest smile, for in spite of Brad, who was definitely allergic to its appeal, she still had some faith in its effect.

'Okay.' Chris smiled back at her, the singularly sweet smile she had noticed at their first meeting.

She made an effort to strengthen the tenuous ties of friendship she had managed to establish between them. 'Haven't you any more pictures to show me?' He shrugged indifferently and made no answer. Jacqui's gaze roved around the bare boards of the floor, to come to rest on a stack of pictures standing in a dark corner. 'May I?' Without waiting for an answer she went to the canvases and began looking through them. Many were unfinished, some no more than a few preliminary sketches of a face or a stretch of water. Then she picked up a landscape painting, and another, and another, that held her undivided attention. For although she possessed no natural talent for painting herself, she was interested in art, and something told her that Chris was a gifted artist with a great future, if he worked at it. For somehow he achieved a magical effect of space and light in these pictures of empty landscapes, lonely beaches and islands empty of people, that she had come to identify with New Zealand paintings of scenery.

'They're very good,' Jacqui murmured slowly, appreciatively. 'Even I can see you've got something. That diffusion of light——'

Suddenly the apathy was gone from his expression. 'That's what I was aiming for!'

'Now this I like!' She picked up another canvas, a scene that seemed to actually generate steam and heat, a rocky landscape with its boiling mud pools beneath a heat-hazed sky. 'It couldn't be anywhere else but Rotorua.' Jacqui laughed. 'Looking at this, I can almost hear the plop-plop of the mud being sucked down into the earth.'

'It must be better than I thought, that picture.'

Jacquie wasn't listening, her attention held by a canvas she had picked up from the pile. She was looking at a portrait of a Maori woman, a face crisscrossed with lines, yet plainly depicting all the dignity and distinction of a proud race. She wore a feather cloak woven from the feathers of the huia, a bird long extinct in the country. The cloak was doubtless an heirloom long cherished, Jacqui mused, like the priceless pendant carved from greenstone in the form of a grotesque little figure, the *tiki*, hanging at her throat.

'She's wearing the *moko*,' Jacqui said in surprise, her gaze held by the scrolls tattooed around mouth and chin of the dark face. 'She must be awfully old.'

'I'll say! I couldn't believe it when someone told me about this very elderly Maori woman, the wife of a chief, who was still living in the district. In the end I ran her to earth in an old *whare*, up in the hills. Interesting bod she turned out to be too. She could remember right back to the time of the Tarawera eruption.' Chris sounded almost animated. 'She didn't want me to paint her portrait, but I promised her it will go to her tribe and won't be sold privately——' he gave a hollow laugh, 'not that she need have worried on that score. I can't imagine the public queueing up to buy my pictures right now.'

'They will, one of these days. You haven't ever had an exhibition of your work?'

He shook his head. 'We're so far out of the way here——'

'That wouldn't have mattered. There's Rotorua——'

'And the family weren't very encouraging, except Mum, that is.'

'Well, I'm sure you've got a gift,' Jacqui said stoutly, 'and it's one you should work at. Have you any more pictures?' Her gaze roved around the shadowy interior with its festoons of spiderwebs in corners of the rough ceiling. All at once she caught sight of a canvas that was turned face to the wall, in the shadows. 'There's another one—over there at the back! Can I see——'

She took a step towards the picture, but for all his slug-
gish air Chris had reached it before her, standing protectively over it, his face contorted with a sort of nervous
anguish. 'No, not that one! Leave it alone!'

She paused. 'It's okay, I just wondered.' She added
encouragingly, 'Why don't you finish the picture on the
easel?'

His voice was apathetic once again. 'Maybe I will,
some time.'

'Well, I think it's a shame!' she said with spirit. 'Anyone
with real talent like you should be working hard all the
time, not just when you feel in the mood.'

Chris moved back towards the couch and dropped
down. 'The others——'

'Never mind what the family say. It's *you*, what you
can do with this gift of yours, that matters!'

Something of her enthusiasm must have got through to
him, she thought, for he said slowly. 'Okay then, I'll give
it another go.' Again the beguiling smile. 'I'll try a portrait
this time—that is, if you'll pose for me.'

'Me?' She was playing for time. 'Why ever me?'

His considering gaze rested on her vivid young face. 'I
reckon I might even come up with something really
worthwhile, if you'd help me.'

She realised his look was the assessing gaze of an artist
and told herself that sitting for a portrait, even if it proved
to be boring, would be a small price to pay for helping
him back to health and maybe eventually making a name
for himself in his chosen profession.

'All right, then.' But she wanted no more mysteries if
they were to be friends. 'I'll make a deal with you. If you
let me see that picture over by the wall——'

He made no answer and, half expecting him to inter-
cept her, she made her way towards the canvas and turned
it up to the light. A girl's face smiled up at her. The girl
in the picture looked happy and carefree, soft fair hair
flowing around her tanned shoulders and the straps of the

blue sun-frock she wore. The same girl who had been in the colour photo pinned to the wall of the cottage, only then she had posed with Nick.

She spoke out of her thoughts. 'I've seen this girl before. It's Lorraine, isn't it? There's a snapshot of her at the cottage at Te Kainga.'

Chris looked startled and she wondered if mention of the girl's name would trigger off another attack of nerves. He said in a choked voice, 'She was with *him*, wasn't she?'

To change the subject, Jacqui said crisply, 'When do you want me to start sitting for my portrait?'

'When?' he echoed vaguely, as if coming back from a long distance.

'I'll come tomorrow, in the afternoon,' she offered, before he could argue the matter. 'Would you like me to wear a special coloured blouse or dress? I've got an emerald green shirt. Or how about a red sweater?'

'No, no,' once again his thin face wore an abstracted expression, 'it's just the face I want to get down on canvas.'

'I can't think why!' Beneath the light words, Jacqui was feeling a deep satisfaction. He really wants to do this portrait, she told herself. Aloud she said, 'It's a date, then!'

She was moving away when his voice arrested her. 'Wait, there's something——'

She turned back to face him. 'What is it?'

'About the picture of you, if I do it, you won't go telling the others up at the house about it? It will be just between you and me, right?'

She nodded. 'If that's the way you want it.'

'I just wanted to be sure.' Chris began sorting out tubes of oil paints.

As she strolled back through the orchard, Jacqui congratulated herself that at least Chris was thinking of making a new start. Maybe with a bit of luck (and help from herself) he might soon be fully recovered in health and too involved in his art to dwell on the past. All he really needed, she mused, was to be given a few words of encouragement and to feel that someone cared about his talent and aspirations. Funny this feeling she had deep down, that somehow she owed it to Chris to help him in any way she could. Because of Nick and Lorraine? But that was ridiculous.

All at once she found herself wondering if Lorraine were the girl who, according to Brad, had accompanied Nick on his air trip to Canada a few weeks previously. Not that one could believe what Brad told her, of course, but remembering the deep antagonism he had for her, merely because she happened to be Nick's sister, she didn't think there could be the slightest doubt in the matter.

CHAPTER FIVE

JACQUI awoke early the next morning to a world drenched in glorious sunshine. This was no day to lie abed, she decided, and soon she was pulling on blue jeans and a scarlet T-shirt. Slipping out of the house, she made her way up the winding hill track. She had come in sight of her destination when a masculine figure appeared around a curve of the track ahead. Brad! Shafts of sunlight were striking gleams in his dark hair and he looked lean and lithe and very attractive—if you didn't know what he was *really* like, of course!

'It's a filly, a little beauty!' Excitement tinged his vibrant tones. 'A chestnut, just like her mother!' The tense angry expression he seemed to keep just for her had vanished, replaced by a look of elation and deep satisfaction. 'Things weren't going along too well up there for a while,' he jerked his dark head towards a paddock further up the rise. 'For a time it was touch and go! But everything's fine now.'

She said wonderingly, 'Have you been up there with the mare all night?'

His big white teeth flashed against the mahogany tan of his face. 'Most of it. Why don't you go on up and take a look? Mother and babe are both doing well.'

'I'll do that!'

She scarcely recognised him in this new exultant mood. Up till now, friendly and forthright though he was with everyone else, with her, a distant enigmatic air had surrounded him. But not today! Clearly in the stress and excitement of the birth of the thoroughbred foal he had quite lost sight of who he was talking to. She happened to be the first person he had encountered this morning and he had to tell someone his news. She couldn't understand why the thought was so depressing.

She watched him go on down the hill, taking the winding path with his easy stride. There was a grace about his movements, no doubt about it. Unconsciously she sighed. If only he would always be like this, relaxed and friendly. But wouldn't that make it rather difficult to remember his true character? To maintain the loathing she felt for him? She pushed the troubling thoughts aside and went on up the slope.

Leaning over the gate, she caught her breath at the sheer beauty of the graceful chestnut mare and her tiny foal. There was something about the small creature that touched her heart. The slender legs were unsteady, its coat glinting golden in the sunlight as it nuzzled the mare.

When she went down the slope she found Pancho waiting for her his soft nicker welcoming her as she fastened the gate behind her. Already it seemed to her that his eyes were brighter and he appeared to be more alert. It was clear that however unpleasant she found her enforced stay at Waiwhetu, to Pancho, the period of sweet fresh grass and suitable medication meant everything. And wasn't that her sole reason for being here?

In the afternoon she wandered down to the stockyards where Rick, his checked scarlet shirt a note of colour, was schooling a young horse. Bernice was perched on the top rail of the fence watching him and Jacqui climbed up to join her.

'Hi, Jacqui.' Rick sauntered over to join the two girls. He pushed his wide-brimmed straw hat to the back of his head. 'Tell me, do you ride?'

She nodded. 'Used to. I'm a bit out of practice right now. If you're wanting someone to exercise your horse, why don't you ask Bernice to oblige?'

'Not me.' Laughing, Bernice shook her head. 'Give me a good old Kiwisaki any time. At least with a farm bike you know where you are. I never did get on well with horses.'

'Over to you!' Rick sent Jacqui a wink. 'Just say the word if you'd like to take a ride right now?'

'Would I ever?' Her blue eyes lighted up. 'With Pancho in sick bay I thought I'd have to wait for ages!'

'I'm your man! Wait there and I'll saddle up Lightning. He's in the corral right now.' He hesitated. 'You did say you're used to the saddle? He's great to ride, but he's got one fault and if you know beforehand——'

Jacqui laughed. 'Try me. Just let me in on his special brand of trouble. Does he bite, kick, rear?'

'Nothing like that. Just the odd time when he gets a fright and shies like mad. But you'll be able to handle him.'

Soon Rick was leading across the yard a young black gelding and while Bernice returned to the house, Jacqui went with Rick to the stables. She patted the horse's black shiny head. 'He looks quiet enough.'

'He is, most of the time—except for that little habit I told you about just when you're off guard. I've had to bail out a few times myself. He's not got his name for nothing!' Rick was throwing a blanket and saddle on the horse, then fastening the girth. 'If you'd rather have one of the other horses I can fetch one from the hill paddock. No problem.'

'No, he'll be fine.' Presently Rick gave her a leg up and she gathered up the reins.

'If you want a really decent ride,' she didn't quite trust the devilry in his eyes, 'you can go thataway,' he indicated a cleared green hill behind the house, 'and you can take a dip in the hot pools over that way. When you hit them.'

Jacqui eyed him suspiciously. 'How long a ride is it?'

'You'll see when you get there. Have a dip for me!'

She couldn't decide whether to believe what he was telling her or not, but just to be on the safe side, she slipped to the ground. 'I'll go and collect my gear.' She was back from the house in a few minutes, her brief blue swimsuit and a towel stuffed into the Air N.Z. travel bag she had slung over her shoulder.

'You did say,' once again Rick helped her up into the saddle, 'that you wanted a good ride?'

'Oh, I do! I do!' It was a long time since she had enjoyed the exhilaration of galloping over the cleared hills of her native country. And on a day like this, with the air incredibly clear, the sky a translucent blue bowl above and the ranges fading away into the distance . . .

Rick watched her ride away. 'Don't forget. Over the hills, through the gullies and you're away laughing, in a hot mud pool!'

'I've got it!' She threw him a farewell smile over her shoulder.

Her mount was evidently accustomed to the procedure of waiting while his rider opened and closed gates, but at last they were out on the green slopes, taking the narrow tracks circling the hills that had been worn by a thousand sheep. Down on the flat ground Jacqui leaned forward in the saddle, urging the gelding to a canter. She revelled in the fresh wind that was blowing across her face and whipping her hair in a dark cloud behind her ears. Presently she set her mount to a gallop and the black steers around them scattered in panic from the pounding hoofs.

Directly ahead she could see a gully where thickly growing flax and tea-tree crowded the trunks of towering native trees. She was about to pull the horse to a slower place when a pukeko rose from the swampy ground underfoot. The next moment there was a flash of iridescent wings before her eyes, then she felt herself flying through the air, to be thrown heavily on the ground.

The force of the impact knocked the breath from her body and for a few minutes she lay motionless, an arm thrown over her eyes, as she struggled for breath.

'Jacqui!' Brad's forceful tones were very close. She took a sneaky look from under her eyelashes to see that he was leaning over her, an expression of anxiety in his eyes. Swiftly, impelled by an instinct she couldn't define, she closed her eyes once again, dark lashes fanning her pale cheeks. The shock of the fall had sent everything else from her mind and she was aware only of Brad, so close she could feel his breath on her face. Vulnerable as she was now, the masculine magnetism against which she had struggled ever since their first meeting, was having its way with her.

'Jacqui! Wake up!' She was aware that he was kissing her gently on the mouth. The thought drifted through her mind that his nearness was very comforting and his kiss was having the oddest effect on her. For a languorous feeling of content pervaded her senses and with that persuasive pressure of his lips on hers she never wanted to break the spell. If only, she mused dreamily, she could stay close in his arms like this for ever.

'Jacqui——' His hands were moving with gentle pressure on her shoulders and she knew it was useless to try to pretend any longer that she had lost consciousness. No use pretending anything really, where Brad was concerned. Pity it couldn't last ... like this. Her hand dropped away from her face and she opened her eyes to meet Brad's concerned look. She made to pull herself up, but his strong arm held her back. 'Take it easy.'

Swiftly she took in the scene around her. The Land Rover standing nearby and the black gelding with reins trailing, cropping the dried grass as though nothing untoward had happened. And Brad ...

'You bailed out on Lightning when he shied like the devil,' he told her. 'A pukeko rose right under his hooves and scared the living daylights out of him. Me too. I happened to come along right behind you just when it all happened. Are you okay?' He released his supporting arm and gingerly she got to her feet, aware all the time of his concerned expression. 'How do you feel?' He was eyeing her intently. 'No bones broken?'

She gave a shaky laugh. 'I guess not. Just,' she added ruefully, 'a sore shoulder and about a hundred odd aches and stiffness all over.'

'Not to worry,' his grin was unexpectedly heart-warming. 'I've got news for you. A special cure for all of that, guaranteed! All you need do is to put yourself in my care for a few hours and you'll be as good as new. You can take my word for it.'

Deep in her mind a warning bell sounded. She mustn't let herself be taken in by his temporary change of attitude towards Nick's scheming young sister.

'*Your* word!' The words came to her lips before she could stop them and in a flash all the goodnatured concern in his face died away, leaving his face aloof and stern. He was angry, very. She knew by the muscle that jerked in his tanned cheek.

'Like I said,' his tone was dangerously quiet, 'if you want to get rid of your stiffness after the fall, I happen to be on the way to a thermal area with hot mineral pools. In case you don't know the area, the pools have got a name for their curative properties. I'll take you there if you want to try them out.' He shrugged broad shoulders. 'It's all the same to me.'

Jacqui hesitated. She was still feeling slightly dazed following her fall and it was an effort to drag her thoughts together. She was fast regaining her previous unflattering opinion of this man. It was much easier to loathe him, she discovered, when he so obviously disliked her, as he did right at this moment. Aloud she explained, 'I was on the way to the hot pools myself——'

'You'd get there in time to come back again.'

She stared at him, wide-eyed. 'But Rick told me ...' Her voice trailed away as she recalled the mischievous glint in Rick's ingenuous blue eyes. 'The brute! And I went and got my swimsuit too!'

A smile tugged at his lips.

'He was having you on! He's got a whacky sense of humour sometimes. But if you really want to go and take a look around, I'll take you.'

His arrogant tone sparked her to say, 'I can still go for a ride on Lightning.' Her glance moved to the black gelding, grazing quietly nearby.

'You reckon?' His heavy dark brows rose satirically. 'With a broken girth?'

She looked at him uncertainly. Was he telling her that just so that he could have her at his mercy and torment her further? She wouldn't put it past him. A glance at the saddle and torn girth lying on the grass not far away, however, confirmed his words.

'Well . . .' She hesitated. The thermal pools sounded exciting and for once she believed what he was telling her, that they would soak away the aches and stiffness from which she was suffering. If only she didn't have to make the journey with him. He took advantage of her indecision by placing two fingers to his lips and emitting a piercing whistle. The sound echoed over the empty hills and had the effect of summoning a rider to the ridge above them. The next moment Bill Lewis came galloping towards them. The stockman's weathered face took on an anxious look as he caught sight of the riderless horse and the saddle lying on the grass.

'Trouble?' His gaze went to Jacqui's pale face.

It was Brad who answered. 'Not too bad,' he replied in his laconic way. 'Jacqui took a toss when Lightning decided to shy. A pukeko flew out of nowhere and scared the hell out of him. He shied like mad and that rotten girth couldn't take the strain. Run him back to the stables for us, will you, Bill?'

'Can do.' His glance returned to Jacqui. 'You're not hurt?'

She laughed reassuringly. 'Don't look so worried Bill! I'm quite all right. It's my dignity that suffered—that is, as well as every bone in my body! But I'll survive. I've taken lots of falls on the farm at home, it's all part of the fun.'

He sent her a relieved grin. 'So long as you're okay.' With a parting wave, he picked up the reins of the grazing horse and began to lead him away.

Brad watched him go, then turned to Jacqui. 'We'd better get cracking.' He had picked up saddle and girth and was throwing them into the Land Rover. Apparently he had lost all interest in her state of health, for he was flinging open the heavy door, saying impatiently, 'Are you coming?'

She must have taken a crack on the head, she reflected, as well as a powerful thumping on back and shoulders, to make her so slow in the uptake. For not until this moment had she realised that she had no choice but to accompany him, other than footing it all the way back to the homestead, that was.

She said with all the dignity she could muster, 'If you insist.' Sarcasm, however, was lost on him, she decided, as she climbed up the high step of the vehicle and sat very straight on the seat while he went around the Land Rover to fold his long length at her side.

'Just wait till I get hold of Rick!' she barely caught his savage mutter as he put his hand to the starter. 'I'll have a piece of him for handing you Lightning as a try-out, and with a girth that was shot to pieces! He must have been out of his skull to do a thing like that!'

'It wasn't his fault,' she protested quickly as they moved over the paddock. 'He did warn me about the shying bit, but I told him I was an experienced rider and I could handle it.'

Brad flicked her a derisive glance. 'You did?'

'Why not?' Stung by the disbelief she read in his eyes, she flung back at him, 'Whatever you think about that accident a while ago, I am used to riding.'

'If you say so.' He couldn't have shown his disbelief more plainly, she thought, fuming. It was there in the ironic twist of the finely chiselled lips, the cool tone of his voice.

Jacqui drew her lips together. She made a mental vow that before she left here for ever she would prove to him her riding ability. She was so enraged she scarcely realised they were entering the filtered light of the bush-filled gully where the branches of great trees met overhead and the tires of the vehicle made little sound on the soft damp earth of the overgrown bush track.

His dominant tones broke across her musing. 'One thing's for sure. After today's little episode you won't be taking out Lightning again—I'll see to that!'

She slanted him a quick glance. Surely he wasn't being considerate of her welfare at last? Not him, not Brad.

'Why?' she demanded hotly. 'Don't you think I can handle him?' As he made no answer she said defensively, 'Anyone can take a tumble when a horse shies unexpectedly. Or could it be,' she asked fiercely, 'that it's your horse that you're worried about?'

'What do *you* think?' His smile, that attractive smile of his, flashed out. After a pause he said mildly, 'Your Pancho seems to be getting along pretty well.'

She mistrusted his sudden change of mood. The thoughts raced wildly through her mind. 'It's time you were getting on your way, young Jacqui.' Could that be what he was getting at? If only she knew!

Aloud, she said brightly, 'Oh, he is, he is! In a week or two he'll be quite different, all the infected places on his coat will be healed up and I'll be able to take him away!'

They were emerging from the moist green world of the gully where trailing branches and creepers brushed the vehicle as they went on. As they shot up a hillside Brad sent her an odd look she couldn't interpret. His eyes seemed to be boring into her. 'Where will you go?'

'I don't know . . . somewhere. I haven't made any plans for the future yet. Maybe I could find some grazing around here and leave him——' She broke off abruptly as the chilling realisation struck her that, according to him, she no longer owned Pancho and therefore had no say in what happened to the horse. She held her breath, for now was his opportunity to put matters right in that direction, say, 'It's over to you, Jacqui.'

He didn't. A laconic 'No hurry' was all the answer she got. All at once she was so angry she could scarcely contain herself and she knew she had to know about Pancho's ownership one way or the other. She would come right out with it and at least then she would know where she stood. The words fell breathlessly from her lips. 'If you still think that Pancho is yours, got a funny idea that you

can take him over because of … you know … what
happened with Nick a while ago——'

'That's right. I do.'

'Well!' The hot colour rushed into her cheeks. 'I think
you're utterly unfair! Just because of Nick, you're penalis-
ing me——'

'No, I'm not.' His coolly rational tone was more maddening than any display of emotion. 'Pancho's yours, you
can do what you like with the horse, but if you want some
advice——'

'I don't!' she muttered half under her breath.

'I'd suggest you leave him with me for a month or so,
until he's back in condition.'

Jacqui was so staggered at his words she could scarcely
believe what she was hearing. 'You're letting me have
him, after all?' she said on an incredulous breath. 'Since
when did you change your mind—about me?'

A flash of white teeth lightened the deep tan of his face.

'Since I saw the way you're taking care of that horse of
yours—and other things.'

Other things? What on earth could he mean? She threw
him a curious glance. 'Such as?'

'Remind me to tell you sometime.

He appeared, however, to have lost interest in the subject, his attention apparently focussed on the steep slope
they were taking.

'I guess I should say "thank you".' It was an effort to
force herself to say the words.

'Why,' Brad bent on her a deep mocking glance, 'when
you wouldn't mean it? What you'd really be telling me is
"It's my horse and he should darn well hand it back to
me". Right?'

It was exactly the observation that had been passing
through her mind. She said huskily, 'Something like that,'
and decided to leave it at that. To change the subject she
said lightly, 'Tell me about these hot pools we're going to.
I suppose they're on your property—like everything else
around here?'

Brad ignored the last few words. 'I lease the area out. A young guy and his wife have just taken over the place. They've got great plans for making the cottage into a tea-room and serving light refreshments for tourists, adding a room they can use as a souvenir shop, running a two-day-a-week bus service to pick up tourists from Rotorua. I told Glenn I'd run him over some fencing materials,' for the first time she noticed the coils of wire and fence battens in the rear of the vehicle, 'so I'll dump them there today.'

'Sounds an interesting sort of place.' They were hurtling down a hillside, sheep scattering in all directions before them, on the way to a bush-filled valley below. At that moment a cloud of silvery spray rose high against the dark backdrop of tree ferns and tea-tree. Jacqui turned to Brad in surprise. 'You didn't tell me there was a geyser down there.'

'I didn't tell you a lot of things about it, but you'll be seeing it all for yourself pretty soon.' They were nearing the valley when Brad swung the vehicle around a sharp bend in the metal track and they came in sight of a blue lake, the limpid waters sparkling with sun-glitter. An old Maori canoe was pulled up under the bushes on the sandy shore and a rowing boat rocked gently at the water's edge. Soon they were dropping down to the lake shore and Brad braked the vehicle at the entrance to a white-painted timber cottage, half concealed by overhanging trees and tall tree-ferns. 'Looks as though they've taken off to town, but no matter.'

Jacqui waited in the Land Rover while he crossed the small verandah, then flung open the door. 'Hi, Glenn! Anyone at home here?'

He was back almost at once. 'Bad luck!' But he didn't *look* disappointed at the emptiness of the house, she thought. He opened the door of the passenger side of the vehicle, sending her a quizzical grin. 'Guess you'll have to put up with me as a guide!'

She dropped lightly down on to the sandy path. 'But you know this area well.'

He nodded. 'Like the back of my hand. I've put up swags of signposts to show the safe routes through the bush. Take a wrong turning on a track and you might find yourself in a pool of boiling water. You'd better stick close to me on the way.'

She looked at him uncertainly. Could he mean——? But his cool gaze was quite impersonal. She must have been crazy to have imagined he could have meant anything but exactly what he said.

Together they strolled past the hibiscus bushes with their brilliant blossoms of orange and scarlet, then paused at the lake's edge. Idly Jacqui watched the brown trout endlessly twisting and turning in the clear water at the lake edge. Brad followed her gaze. 'Easy to see they're used to being fed by whoever has the cottage.'

Jacqui's gaze moved over the stretch of shimmering water to the hills on the opposite shore. She could glimpse narrow paths winding over silica banks and wisps of steam rising from among the densely growing tea-tree.

He came to stand beside her, so close that she could feel the warmth of his shoulder through his thin cotton-shirt. 'Looking for that hot pool I promised you? Don't worry— I'll take you to the best swimming place you've ever stepped into. Actually it's an ancient volcanic cavern with a jade-green pool way down in the depths. How does that strike you?

She eyed him laughingly. 'It sounds to me just the place where there are lots of bats and glowworms——'

'Only at night. And I did warn you,' he mocked softly, 'about sticking close to me.' Before she could answer he was running on, 'I've named it Emerald Cave and it's somewhere that's quite unspoiled. I'm going to make certain it stays that way! No one gets the lease for this area from me unless I'm satisfied they aren't going to make any changes in the surroundings.'

'You like everything to be natural?' She spoke unthinkingly.

'Oh, definitely!' There was a warm, compelling note in

his voice and taken by surprise, she looked swiftly upwards
to meet his gaze. For a timeless moment, a magic current
locked their gaze together. It was very still, the air
pervaded by a sensuous warmth. Then abruptly Brad
turned away. 'Shall we go?' His tone was as cool as ever
and as he moved towards the dinghy Jacqui wondered if
she had imagined that crazy moment of togetherness.
Moments like that just didn't happen, not really, not between her and Brad. They couldn't stand the sight of each
other, could they? With an effort of will she wrenched her
mind back to the deep vibrant tones. 'Glenn's got ideas of
running a jet boat on the lake to ferry tourists over to the
other side, but the dinghy will do us for today.'

'Yes,' Jacqui agreed faintly. She was fighting a traitorous urge that threatened to take possession of her. It must
surely be something to do with the sense of isolation, as if
they were the only two people in the whole world, the soft
warm air—but whatever the cause, she *must* resist this
dangerous sense of languorous content *with the wrong man*.
Still, the madness persisted, despite her efforts to resist its
insidious power. She couldn't seem to tear her gaze away
from Brad's lean muscular body as he dipped the oars.
Trailing a hand in the sun-splintered water, she told herself once again that she must surely have suffered a severe
jolt on the head in that fall she had taken back there.
Otherwise she would be able to fight her way out of the
sense of wild sweet happiness that threatened to take
over.

Presently he tied the boat up at a jetty where a track
curved away through the waving fronds of punga trees.
He took her arm to help her out of the boat and on to the
landing. And that too was a mistake, Jacqui realised at
once, as the touch of his hand on her bare skin sent a
shiver of excitement running along her nerves.

Presently they were taking a narrow track, overgrown with ferns and five-finger and tea-tree, the pink
and white silica of the path twisting upwards through
the lush undergrowth. Ahead was the wild yet delicate

scent of starry white manuka blossoms. As they climbed higher, she caught the plop-plop of gurgling mud pools and the air was humid with steam rising from the volcanic hot springs. Then at last they reached a cleared rocky flat and she pushed back the tendrils of hair clinging damply to her forehead, and gazed down at the beautifully tinted terraces below. Half obscured by drifting steam rising from boiling pools of murky green, framed by tree-ferns, the terraces were daubed by nature's paint brush in pink and green and orange of wet and shining silica.

'Fantastic!' Jacqui breathed, taking in the colourful spectacle. 'I bet you called it Rainbow Terraces?'

'What else?' Brad was climbing a still higher slope and she went to join him on a pink silica path that was barely wide enough for two people to walk together.

Smilingly, she glanced up into his lean brown face. 'Where next?'

Immediately she chided herself for that smile. Somehow today she kept forgetting who he was—and who she was, for that matter. It was a habit that seemed to be growing on her. She tried to infuse an impersonal note into her happy tones. 'You couldn't do better than that?'

'I could, you know! Along this track there are so many hot springs I've given up trying to count them.' Brad led her on as they made their way through the moist heat of steam-clouded overhanging bush. A fantail flitted along beside them, the wings brushing their heads, as they pushed their way through creepers and trailing branches. Then suddenly they were looking down on an expanse of pewter-coloured silica, the surface broken by clear pools of green with their boiling thermal waters.

Jacqui leaned on the railings, watching the many craters forming fantastic patterns in the mud. 'It's a bit awe-inspiring——'

'And dangerous. It doesn't pay to go off the path anywhere around here. That's why,' his voice deepened, 'I'm keeping a tight hold of you, young Jacqui.'

She knew only too well the effect his touch had on her and some instinct warned her to jerk herself free. The attempt to escape him, however, was useless, for he merely held her arm in a tighter grip.

'I'm all right,' she said stiffly, 'I don't need to be *held*!' With a sideways jerk she wrenched herself free. 'It doesn't look all that dangerous to me down there. The edge looks as hard as a rock.'

'You'd better take my word for it!' His dominant masculine tone nettled her and driven by a devil of retaliation, she dropped lightly down the bank. The moment her feet touched the wet grey surface she felt with horrified amazement, the silica crumbling away beneath her. In another minute—just in time the horror was avoided as Brad, his feet firmly planted on the bank, leaned forward to swing her up in his arms and carry her back to safety.

'You crazy little fool!' His harsh tones penetrated her whirling senses.

She was still shuddering with the horror of it all. The deceptively firm surface and the boiling pool bubbling below. The next moment rememberance of the dangerous moments blended into excitement of a different sort for Brad was holding her so close she could feel the firm pressure of his muscular chest against her soft body. Her heart was thudding wildly and she knew it wasn't because of the danger, not the silica sort of danger anyway.

'What the hell were you thinking of, doing a crazy thing like that?' But how could she think of anything, with his face so close to hers, his arms around her?

'I'll believe you next time,' she whispered shakily.

'You'd better!' His voice was so low she barely caught the grated words.

He set her down and she went to lean over the railings, her thoughts racing confusedly. If only it had been any other man but Brad who had come to her rescue! It was mean of fate to arrange matters this way, because now she found herself indebted to him once again. She couldn't even explain away the stupid thing she had done, because thank heaven he had no way of knowing the effect his touch had on her. She couldn't imagine why he affected her this way, but it was very hard to fight against the effect of his nearness. It wasn't as if it *meant* anything, she told herself, it was just that he happened to possess an aura of masculine attraction that was challenging and exciting—and definitely dangerous!

'Still want that swim in a pool?' His quirky grin told her that his brief anger had evaporated.

'More than ever.'

Presently they were turning off the track into a path leading down a slope and soon they were taking the rough earth steps cut between fern-studded banks, picking their way over twisted tree roots that snaked over damp earth and moss. The steps, Jacqui thought, seemed to lead downwards for ever, but at last Brad paused beside her. 'That's it—Emerald Cave!' Even in her turmoil of conflicting emotions she was struck by the sight. Sunlight filtered through the lacy green of the tall punga trees rising at the entrance to a great cavern. Ferns clung to the curving rock walls and below she caught the glimmer of water, still and dark and green.

'The warm pool I promised you.' Brad was standing close. 'Recommended as a cure for all sorts of problems. Let's try it out, shall we?' The thoughts raced through her mind. What did he mean, she wondered, by 'problems'? Two people who loathed each other yet—She pushed the thoughts aside and said brightly, 'I've brought along my swimsuit! This looks as good a place as any to change.' She made her way to the bushes growing thickly at the side of the cavern. A few minutes later she stuffed her clothing beneath a tree trunk and stepped out of the shelter.

She found Brad waiting for her. Wearing brown swimming trunks of the same tint as his skin, he was staring down into the pool. Slim-hipped and broad-shouldered, he looked lithe and muscular, she mused, and really very attractive, if you cared for that type.

On the wet muddy path with its twisting tree roots, he put out a hand to help her down the slippery slope, and this time she made no attempt to resist him. Steam was rising from the still green depths and as she slid into the pool the silky texture of the water bubbling up from a spring deep underground was like a caress, giving her an instant feeling of well-being. She smiled across at Brad—somehow today it was difficult to remember not to smile at him—'How deep is the pool?'

He was treading water beside her. 'No one knows the answer to that one. The Maoris have always known about the cavern, but they avoided it, believed it was the home of the *taniwha*——'

Jacqui nodded. 'I know. The sea-dragon in his underground cavern——'

'Who's supposed to lurk in bottomless pools like this one. Hence the old name for the place, I guess, "Forbidden Cave". Mind you, it's very deep and who knows,' his tone was teasing, 'what monster surfaces here at night? Maybe the Maoris in the early times had something, at that. One could believe anything of a place like this!'

'On a day like today,' her heart answered. The moist heat, the stillness, was casting a spell over her. Or could it be Brad who was making her feel this way, Brad whom she hated, should hate, did—— Clamping down firmly on her errant thoughts, she pulled a face and said lightly, 'First it was bats in the cave, now its a fearsome *taniwha*. Are you trying to scare me away?'

His vibrant glance held hers. 'Could I?'

'Not with you around.' The words came without her volition, but fortunately he didn't appear to have heard them.

'Come with me,' he was saying, 'and I'll take you into an entrance that leads into another pool——' He swam to one side of the cavern and she followed him, their strokes as they cleaved the water making little sound. In the soft warm thermal pool Jacqui was finding it difficult to make progress. It was as if her whole body were weighted.

Brad guided her through the narrow entrance, then they were in another cavern, dark, mysterious and utterly silent. They waded to the edge and she leaned against a rock, looking up at the curving walls where moss, ferns and climbing plants clung to the damp surface. 'It's so quiet,' she breathed, 'you feel scared to speak in case you break the spell.'

'Think so?' His laughing face was in shadow. 'You'd be surprised at the acoustics of this place. How about a demonstration like someone singing?'

The next moment, the words of an old Maori love song fell around her. How could his authoritative voice be so low and seductive?

'When I look at you
You turn your face away
Though in your heart, dear,
I know you love me.'

'Love me . . .' the words echoed back from the great rock walls around them.

Brad moved close to her, so close that her breath was coming unevenly. 'I see what you mean.'

He said very low, 'Do you, Jacqui?'

'About the echo,' she added hastily.

'Who cares about the echo!'

It was no use. A force stronger than hate or contempt or resolution was taking over, and she found herself swaying towards him, to be enfolded in strong arms, his body pressed to hers. Her arms crept around his shoulders, then his lips claimed hers and a wild pulsing sweetness carried her away into a world she hadn't known existed.

When at last he released her, the steam rising in the green gloom of the cave obscured his face and she couldn't read his expression. She decided, however, that he appeared much the same as usual. Maybe he was in the habit of kissing girls in caves, even girls he thoroughly disliked. Suddenly all the magic of the last few moments drained away, and she turned away. 'It's a bit—enervating. I'm going out.'

Brad's voice was tinged with a wicked amusement. 'The pool, you mean?'

'What else?' She managed to produce a fairly carefree smile, then began swimming over the pool towards the narrow break in the rocks.

Presently, in the shelter of the bushes at the side of the cavern, she towelled herself dry. Perversely, now that she had achieved her objective, she wished herself back in the sensuous warmth of the hidden cave, regretted having shattered the intimacy of those moments with Brad. Just a kiss, so why was she so bemused? How could she be so shaken by a caress from a man for whom she had nothing but contempt?

Did it show, she wondered, the sense of excitement that was still with her, the soft dreamy look of a girl who had been kissed by a man to whom, why not admit it, she was wildly, crazily attracted? She had longed for that kiss to go on for ever, no matter where it might lead, so long as it was Brad, whom she loved—Love! She brought herself up with a jerk. But she hated him! What in heaven's name was she thinking of to let her thoughts drift in that direction. Blame the intimacy of the surroundings. She would *make* herself think of those moments in the gloom as a nothing thing, just as he no doubt regarded them, a momentary impulse born of the isolation of the forbidden cave with its deep hidden fires.

She was silent as he rowed the dinghy back over the lake to the opposite shore. Because she was determined not to let herself surrender to the physical attraction he had for her, because of course that was all it was, she forced her gaze away from him. Think of Nick, she told herself. It worked, it really worked! For all at once she felt mad with Brad, with herself too. For how could she have been so weak as to surrender so warmly to his idle caress?

He pulled the boat up on the shore and they strolled

together towards the cottage. 'Looks as though there's no one turned up there yet!' His tone was quite impersonal, just as though there had been no instinctive fusion of their lips in the cave. Well, if that was the way he wanted it, that suited her fine. She brought her mind back to the deep masculine tones. 'I'll get this stuff unloaded. Here's the key of the cottage,' he held it out, 'you might want to freshen up.'

Jacqui shook her head. 'I'll wait down by the lake.'

She strolled back to the shore, her gaze moving over the scene around her. Wisps of steam rose from the manuka bush nearby and the lake water was a sheet of rippling blue silk, so clear she could see the brown trout swimming near the shore. At that moment a black swan glided past. She saw it all with only half her mind, conscious only of Brad who was unloading fencing from the Land Rover and tossing it in a heap beside the cottage. Probably, she mused, he disliked her now even more than ever, if that were possible, but what did she care? In an effort to rally her spirits she thought hard about Nick.

Brad was back before long, to drop down on the warm grass. 'Refreshments coming up!' He was tipping out the contents of the cardboard carton he had carried from the vehicle. 'Mrs Beeson takes a pride in rustling up man-sized sandwiches—try one!' He proffered the packet of sandwiches wrapped in clear plastic. In spite of the out-door activities of the day, however, Jacqui found she had no appetite, but she nibbled a sandwich and sipped the mug of hot coffee he had poured from the flask.

When they had finished the snack, he leaned back on the grass regarding her, hands crossed behind his head. 'Care to take a look through the cottage while you're here?'

'No, no.' Some instinct of danger made her answer instinctively. Run, girl, get away while you can! With a glance at her wrist-watch she said lightly, 'I've got to get back. I'm late as it is!'

'You're joking!' His deep compelling gaze held hers.

All at once the soft warm air, the sense of utter isolation, had its way with her and she had the odd feeling that there was nothing in all the world but Brad's magnetic gaze . . . like deep pools where one could drown . . . if one weren't careful. With an effort she fought her way back to sanity. If he imagined that merely because of those moments of madness in the cave—somehow she had to remove from his mind any mistaken ideas he might have regarding her ardent response to his caresses, and all at once she knew just how she could do it.

'It's Chris,' she said crisply. 'I promised to meet him this afternoon in his studio. He'll be wondering what's happened to me.'

He sat up abruptly. 'Chris!' He rapped out the name, steel in his tone.

'That's right,' she flung him a glittering smile. 'He wants to see me specially about something.'

'I get it!' His stare was disconcerting and she knew she had settled the score for his disturbing kiss. She was fast learning to read the strong intelligent face, and clearly the boss wasn't at all pleased about his young brother's friendship with her. One would have imagined, she thought hotly, that Brad would be glad that Chris had begun to show an interest in life once again, but it seemed that nothing she could do would please him.

She flung around to face him, eyes bright with defiance and anger. 'You don't approve of Chris being friendly with me? Or should I say,' she added angrily, 'with Nick's sister?'

'I didn't say so.'

'You didn't need,' she said in a low tone, 'to spell it out. Anyway,' she demanded with spirit, 'what's wrong with me?'

'Nothing at all!' There was an edge to his drawling voice. 'On the contrary, you happen to be very attractive. Didn't any man ever tell you?' His mocking gaze went to her vulnerable young face, to move to her soft lips and down to the apricot-tan of her skin where sunlight had touched the hollows of her throat.

What an admission, and from *him*! Jacqui felt the hot colour rush into her cheeks and her heart began to thud ridiculously.

'But it's what my kid brother thinks about you that matters!'

Oh, she should have known that he wouldn't be handing out any compliments in her direction, only the two-edged kind!

She realised he was coolly regarding her, his lips curved in a half-mocking smile. '*To all appearances* you're beautiful and warm and sweet, and young Chris is no different from any other man.'

From you? The words rose to her lips, but something in his dispassionate glance daunted her.

'He's an odd sort of guy,' she wrenched her mind back to his tones, 'up and down like a yo-yo and gets depressed as hell when things go wrong. The state he's been in lately it wouldn't take much to push him right over the edge, so—just go easy with him where the love games are concerned, will you? Do I make myself clear?'

His arrogant tone sparked off her anger anew. 'So I'm to keep my distance from Chris, is that it? It wouldn't even occur to you,' she cried passionately, 'that I might be able to help him! He doesn't seem to be getting on too well here by himself! Whatever you say, I know he needs me——'

'Is that so?' His mocking tone was infuriating to her taut nerves. 'Tell me, just how do you propose carrying out this welfare work of yours?'

'I'll tell you——' Just in time she recalled her promise to Chris to keep secret his revival of interest in art that was her sole reason for her visits to him in the old shed in the orchard. Instead she burst out, 'I don't know what you're worrying about! Chris is old enough to look after himself, and if it's because of me, I'll only be staying for a short time, remember?'

His glance was enigmatic. 'Long enough, I'd say, to do a lot of damage, when it comes to young Chris.'

'You're wasting your time lecturing me,' she said with spirit. 'Your brother is still carrying a torch for someone else, anyone can see that. Just because she's gone away——'

'And whose fault,' he cut in tersely, 'is that?'

'I know all about that,' she cried defensively, 'and if you're getting at Nick again—My goodness, he could hardly have abducted the girl. She must have liked him a lot!'

Brad swung around abruptly. 'Let's go, shall we?' His voice was harsh with anger. He strode back towards the Land Rover and she hurried along beside him. Soon she was climbing into the vehicle and he slid in the driver's seat, to start the motor with a savage jerk.

They sped along the track and hurtled into the main road. Soon they were running over cleared green hillsides as Brad, abandoning the tracks he had followed on the way to the thermal area, drove over the paddocks, scattering sheep in all directions, to take steep slopes and run down the other side.

In the uneasy silence Jacqui's thoughts raced confusedly. One half of her mind was saying, 'Stupid, stupid, now you've ruined everything!' The other, the sensible part, 'But I had to, I had to or I'd find myself falling in love with him, and I couldn't risk that happening!'

Only as they turned into the winding track in the gully did Brad drop to a lower speed. Now, however, Jacqui was feeling too incensed with him to be aware of the cool damp fragrance of the bush all around. All she wanted was to escape from Brad's disturbing presence. So she continued to sit very straight in her seat and to gaze determinedly ahead.

CHAPTER SIX

JACQUI had leaped down from the Land Rover to open
and close the last gate before they reached the homestead
when she caught sight of Sue. The other girl was taking
her thoroughbred gelding over the jumps in the grassy
enclosure by the stables. When the Land Rover drew up
in the yards, Sue came strolling towards them, the sun
making a nimbus around her ash-blonde hair.

'Thank heaven you're back, Brad!' Jacqui she ignored
completely. 'I need your help. Drum's developing a bad
habit of baulking at the jump and I can't get him out of
it.' Her red lips curved in a dazzling smile. 'Guess he
needs a man's hand to sort him out. Someone like you
who he knows means business!'

'Leave him to me.' Brad dropped to the ground and
soon he and Sue were deep in conversation. How could
Sue maintain her perfection of appearance, Jacqui
wondered, with scarcely a blonde hair out of place and
not a dirt stain on her white shirt or immaculate jodhpurs
even in the dusty enclosure with its makeshift jumps of
painted oil drums and pieces of timber? Or could it be,
she mused, that the other girl allowed nothing to mar her
appearance at a time when Brad was expected back at
the homestead? What did it matter anyway? She and the
boss hated each other. Why *must* she need to keep reminding herself of that all-important fact!

A few minutes later, as the other two showed no signs
of finishing their engrossing chat together, Jacqui slipped
down from the vehicle and with a brief murmur of
'Thanks' to Brad, she hurried away. It was late in the
day, she realised now. How could the hours have fled by
so swiftly? But Chris would still be waiting for her in the
shed, she reassured herself. He might even have attempted

some preliminary background work on the portrait he
intended painting of herself. When she arrived at the shed,
however, she found the door closed and, pushing it open,
she found the place was empty. Chris must have become
tired of waiting for her after all. Nor was he in the living
room or lounge when she went into the house. Oh well,
she would see him at dinner tonight and explain to him
what had happened today to cause her not to keep their
appointment. She showered, changed into a filmy dress in
muted pink and blue tonings and slipped her feet into
cool white sandals.

Later, however, when she went into the lounge room a
swift glance told her that Chris hadn't yet arrived.

Brad, freshly showered and shaved, was standing by
the cocktail cabinet. Even in the casual gear of short-
sleeved brilliantly patterned Polynesian-style cotton shirt
and cream slacks, he looked, she thought, very much the
master of this vast estate. How easily she could let herself
be fooled by him, this man with his aura of power and
arrogant good looks. Sue stood at his side, her tall blonde
elegance a perfect foil for his virile male figure. The two
were laughing together and looking in her direction.

Jacqui went to drop to a low stool beside Bernice who,
in her usual fashion, had perched herself on the arm of
Rick's chair. She was leaning towards him, a soft adoring
expression in her dark eyes.

'For you, Jacqui.' Brad had crossed the room to bring
her a sherry, his pleasantly impersonal tone betraying no
hint of their recent stormy encounter. She might just as
well have been any casual girl visitor here, she thought
crossly. She decided it was a game at which two could
play and forcing her voice to a non-commital note she
said, 'Thank you,' and looked him straight in the eye.

'I guess you could do with a drink.' Sue had come to
stand beside Brad. For once, Jacqui thought, the other
girl had acknowledged her presence in the room. 'I mean,'
Sue ran on meaningfully, 'after all that kerfuffle about
you today.'

'So you heard about Jacqui taking a toss?' Bill Lewis put in. His weathered face broke into a grin. 'The boss put on a big rescue act today,' he explained to the room at large, 'arrived bang on time to rescue a maiden in distress. Hey, Brad!' he appealed to Brad, busy at the cocktail bar, 'how come you knew just when to arrive on the scene?'

Jacqui wished that Bill would drop the subject of her fall today. She shot a glance towards Brad, whose attention appeared to be taken up with the drink he was mixing. 'No sense in leaving her waiting around until you got around to doing something about it,' he said laconically. 'You're the guy whose job it is to patrol the fences. I had to whistle you up from heaven only knows where.'

At last Jacqui found her voice. 'I'm not a lost sheep or something,' she protested.

'No reflections on you, Jacqui,' Bill told her with twinkling eyes. He turned towards Sue. 'What do *you* think, Sue? Now that's something you never thought of, staging a big rescue act.'

Sue's lips were tightly compressed and Jacqui suspected the blonde beauty wasn't accustomed to any other girl gaining the masculine attention she took as her due.

'Wished you'd come up with something like that yourself, huh?' said Bill, grinning.

She shot her tormentor a loaded glance. It was Bernice who said laughingly, 'I'll have to think about that one! What do you say, Rick? Would you carry me off to the Emerald Cave if you came upon me looking all helpless and pale and haggard, lying flat out on the grass?'

'I wasn't!' Jacqui protested, but no one was listening.

'First find your pukeko,' Rick grinned, 'then you can think about your man!'

Everyone laughed except Sue who, Jacqui noticed, was frowning angrily. After that, to Jacqui's immense relief, the subject was dropped.

Rick got up to pour himself a drink, pulling a wry face as he passed Jacqui. 'Did Brad tear a strip off me when he got back today for sending you out on Lightning!'

Jacqui laughed. 'It wasn't your fault, and you did warn me. If only you'd warned me about the pukeko too!'

Sue's deep tones, with their note of deceptive sweetness, echoed around the room. 'I thought you said you could ride, Jacqui? You'll have to get Rick to give you some lessons on riding and caring for your gear as well,' she observed silkily. 'I mean, one horse is enough to damage with sheer neglect without coming to grief on another one.' She sipped her drink. 'You seem to have quite a knack for it!'

Jacqui's mouth felt stiff. 'It was an accident,' she said defensively. 'It was just lucky for me that Brad happened to come along right afterwards.'

'Very lucky!' Sue gazed into her golden sherry. 'A good chance for Brad to show you around the area—did you have a dip in the Emerald Cave?'

'Yes, we did.' Such an ordinary statement, so why did Jacqui feel so ridiculously selfconscious? In the sudden silence in the room it seemed to her as if everyone were listening and to her horror she felt the hot colour creeping over her face. Brad, busy at the bar, appeared to be unaware of the conversation echoing around him. Her gaze moved to Sue and she caught an odd expression in the other girl's eyes. Suspicion, anger and something else, something cruel and menacing. The next moment, watching the lovely laughing face as Sue turned to speak with Bill, Jacqui wondered if she had merely imagined that fleeting look.

'Next time you're wanting a ride,' she brought her mind to Bill's fatherly tones, 'pass the word along to me and I'll fix you up with one of my mounts. I've got a notion you can handle a horse as well as anyone!'

'I wouldn't trust her with Drum!' said Sue with her flashing smile, and only Jacqui caught the hint of malice behind the light words.

Help came from an unexpected quarter. 'Why not?' came Brad's lazy drawl.

Jacqui tried not to look as though the talk concerned herself.

'Well——' for the first time in their acquaintance, Jacqui thought, Sue appeared to be at a loss for words, but she recovered herself quickly. 'Just that she's an unknown quantity around here.'

'Oh, I don't know.' Puzzled and surprised, Jacqui glanced across to meet Brad's lingering gaze. 'At least she knows how to bail out without too much damage.'

She didn't know whether to take this as a compliment or not.

'Only to her horse,' Sue said mockingly, and everyone laughed. Jacqui, however, had caught the derisive twist of the girl's lips and knew she had an enemy, although what she had done to cause the enmity she couldn't imagine. To her vast relief, the next moment the housekeeper announced dinner and the group moved into the dining room.

'Have you seen anything of Chris?' Jacqui whispered, as the woman came to the table.

'Not all day. It's no use worrying about that one, though. I suppose he'll turn up again for meals in his own good time, he always does. No wonder he's so thin!' She put down on the table a hot vegetable dish filled with roasted kumeras.

When the meal had come to an end and everyone else seemed to have drifted away, Jacqui went along the passage and gave a knock on Chris's door. After a moment's delay, a voice called 'Come in,' and she went into the room. Chris was sitting on his bed, looking up at her with dull eyes.

'Sorry about today.' She crossed the room to stand smiling down at him. 'I went to the thermal pools with Brad and you know how it is over there. There's so much to see, the time just slipped by. I did try to get back in time.'

'It doesn't matter.' He seemed scarcely interested in her explanation.

'But it does! What about the painting——?'

He shrugged apathetically. 'Forget it.'

'That's just what I don't want to do. Look, I'm going to be at the shed tomorrow, early, no matter what. Is it okay with you?'

Once again he shrugged thin shoulders. 'If you like.' He turned his face away from her. 'If you don't mind——'

There seemed nothing more she could say. 'Would you care for something to read?' she offered inadequately. 'I've got some London magazines and there are lots of features on art——'

He only shook his head and Jacqui felt a rush of irritation. If only he would snap out of these dark moods instead of surrendering himself to loneliness and despair!

She was closing the door behind her when Sue and Brad came strolling along the hall towards her. Evidently they were bound for the pool outside, for both wore swimsuits. Her hand still resting on the door handle, Jacqui's startled gaze took in the surprised glances of the other two. The boss's dark closed expression left no doubt as to his feelings at seeing Jacqui emerging from Chris's room. As to his companion, Sue's face wore a look of smug satisfaction and her lips curled contemptuously. The next moment, as the couple moved past her, Sue's strong tones drifted back along the passage. 'Looks like Chris has found himself a new playmate. Oh well, it might be a good thing for him at that. Might take his mind off himself and his problems. Funny, isn't it, that he's such a hopeless picker when it comes to choosing girl-friends!'

Later, lying in bed, Jacqui couldn't seem to wrench her thoughts away from Sue—and Brad. Her eyes were fixed on the novel she was attempting to read, but her mind saw only Sue's face as the other girl gazed up at Brad with her provocative smile. Probably Brad would kiss the other girl in the pool tonight, Jacqui mused irritatedly. Sue, well versed in the arts of love, would be expert at hiding her true feelings. Never would she give herself away as Jacqui had done today. For Brad must have known that when it came to his touch, her defences were down and that she had been swept away—well, almost—by feelings that were new to her. In the past she had found it easy to call the tune in a love affair. Always she had been the one to keep a cool head. It had been so easy for her—but then never before had she met a man like Brad.

The night was still and moonlit, a perfect evening for a dip in water sunwarmed through long hours of daylight. At intervals she caught drifts of laughter from the pool, then after a time there were only two voices. She recognised Brad's vibrant tones and Sue's peals of laughter. Why couldn't *she* have laughed with him in the warm intimacy of Emerald Cave, instead of responding passionately to his caress? One thing was sure—restlessly she punched her pillow—she wouldn't let herself be lured into the trap again! Two kisses from Brad had been more than enough to cause her to forget all about Nick. She had best watch herself, the man was a positive danger!

She awoke the next morning feeling unaccountably restless and after breakfast was over she slipped away and let herself into the shed that Chris used as a studio. She'd had a thought that maybe if the place had a more cheerful and inviting appearance he might be inspired to return to work. She was standing on a chair, cleaning a window, when she caught the sound of footfalls on the path outside and the next minute Chris flung open the wide doors. Jacqui met his surprised look with an engaging smile. 'Just some cleaning-up operations!'

'I get it.' The thought ran through her mind that today he appeared infinitely more relaxed. Maybe the bad days would become fewer and fewer as time went by.

His gaze was roving around the room. 'No cobwebs, and it all looks so damned tidy!' He looked at her suspiciously. 'You haven't touched my paints or pictures?'

'No, no, nothing like that,' she assured him. 'I just got rid of the dust, made things look a bit more liveable-in.' Cunningly she added, 'Now that you're using the place as a studio again, you'll need room to move.'

Already, however, it seemed to her that Chris had lost interest in her tidying-up activities. He was shifting the easel to a position nearer to the window, drawing aside the tattered curtains.

'Isn't it a bit dark in here for painting?' She made to open doors he had closed behind him, but his shout of protest arrested her.

'No!' he muttered angrily. 'I don't want them poking their noses into my business, telling me I should be out on the run.'

She looked at him wonderingly. 'Would Brad do that?'

He gave a nervous laugh. 'I wouldn't put it past him. They all think my art efforts are a heck of a big joke. They don't believe I've got anything in me.' His face fell and he bit his lip. 'The only one who cheered me on was Lorraine. When I lost her I guess I lost the inclination, if you get me.'

Jacqui asked, surprised, 'Was she an art student?'

'Good grief no, nothing like that, but she—believed in me.'

'So do I!'

'You?' His smile was indulgent. 'What would you know about art, Jacqui?'

'Nothing really,' she confessed, 'but I used to room with a girl who was an art student and,' she added stoutly, 'I do know good work when I see it, and there's a certain technique about your work. It's different from anyone else's——'

'Oh, I'll grant you that,' he observed on a harsh laugh.

'It's unique,' she persevered, 'there's something about it. I can't explain what I'm getting at,' she threw up a hand in a helpless gesture, 'but you'll see that I'm right one of these days.'

'Maybe. Well, I'd better get cracking.' Chris went to tear down wisps of curtain from a high window, letting in the bright early-morning sunlight. Then he stood still, regarding her, with an assessing expression. 'There's just one thing——' The next minute he had caught her long hair and twisted it high in a topknot. 'Can you make it stay that way? Here,' he was flinging open a drawer in a bureau, to pull out a Spanish comb, 'this should do the job!' To Jacqui he seemed to have changed into an entirely different man, with confidence and assertiveness taking the place of his customary diffidence and self-doubt.

'Just as you say—sir!' Laughing, she fastened the comb in the knot on the top of her head. She pulled a face at him. 'Now all I need is a big fan!' Chris was busy squeezing paint on to a palette, however, and took no notice.

Soon he was working with swift clean strokes an an hour later Jacqui rose from her chair to stretch cramped limbs. 'You know, I wouldn't do this "sitting" act for anyone else. You've just got to make a success of the portrait——' She broke off, for as Chris stood aside she gained a clear view of the sketched-in picture, that already had taken on an amazing likeness. 'But I'm not really like that——' The words came unbidden to her lips, for the girl in the picture had about her a radiance, a soft glowing look. Like a girl in love—she brought her thoughts up with a jerk.

'It's the way I see you.' Once again she was aware of the confident tone of an artist who, though self-taught and unacknowledged, knew himself to be a master of his craft. He stared at Jacqui through narrowed eyes. 'What's wrong? Don't you like it? It's not what you'd call a true picture?'

'Yes, I suppose it is,' she said hesitantly, reluctant to admit even to herself that the portrait showed her as she really was and whether she admitted it to herself or not, made no difference. The thought was so staggering, so unexpected, she felt crushed by it. The next minute she told herself that the idea was ridiculous, she had merely imagined that expression in her face. How stupid could you get?

As the week went by the days fell into a pattern. Afternoons Jacqui spent in the studio, posing for her por-

trait while Chris painted, mornings she was busy tending
Pancho. Each day brought an improvement in the horse's
condition, and next week she planned to start exercising
him. Soon after that she would be on her way. Odd how
the thought brought no particular joy. She should be
looking forward to escaping from this enforced stay, only
somehow she wasn't. It must be because of Chris and his
portrait of herself, she told herself. Not only the portrait,
but the scheme she had in mind for arranging a display of
his work in Rotorua. He was working long hours in the
studio and soon he would be putting the finishing touches
to the portrait.

Between the two of them, she and Chris had succeeded in
keeping the picture a secret. The family had become accustomed to her daily visits to the old shed in the orchard
and took them as a matter of course. All except Brad,
whom she had passed once or twice on her way to the
studio. He had greeted her with a brief inclination of his
dark head, his gaze cold and unsmiling. At other times
when she happened to be with Chris, idly dancing to the
strains of the stereo after dinner, or leaving the room with
him to stroll up an incline in the dusk, she was acutely aware
of Brad's brooding glance. Clearly the boss wasn't at all
pleased at his young brother's new friend. Great! Brad's
tight-lipped glance had the effect of making her all the
more determined to continue her relationship with Chris.
She didn't have to go along with Brad's wishes, even if
everyone else at the station appeared to regard him as
some sort of overlord, She owed him nothing—except the
brief stay in his home, a voice in her mind reminded her.
A small debt, she told herself, when you knew all that he
owed Nick for the way he had treated him. And anyone
who harmed her brother she would never forgive. Surely
Brad must recognise that by now. She had made it plain
enough, heaven knows. Her cheeks burned at the thought
of his kiss in the cave. Well, most of the time.

Today when she reached the shed, closing the doors
behind her and taking her usual position, Chris had a

dazzling smile for her. Plainly he was at the end of his portrait.

'Just a few more touches,' he told her a little later, 'and that's it! I've got to call a halt somewhere.' His face wore the abstracted look of an artist deeply involved in his work. 'Otherwise I'll keep adding bits and altering until I've ruined the whole thing.'

'You're really pleased with it, aren't you?' She got up from her seat at last to stand beside him, studying the finished portrait. Familiarity with the picture had dulled the first impression and she refused to entertain that initial thought that the eyes of the girl in the picture betrayed secrets too unbelievable to contemplate.

'I don't know,' she brought herself back to Chris's thoughtful tones. 'I can see plenty of faults in it.'

'Don't tell me,' she chided, 'I know the breed. You artists are never really satisfied with anything you paint.'

'We wouldn't get much farther if we were.' He grinned and she realised that for the first time in their acquaintance he was speaking in the manner of a professional artist. Goodness, she thought, her portrait must be good to have given him this new confidence in his artistic capabilities. The knowledge gave her the opportunity to say, 'So I guess you're about ready to show some of your work!' Before he could protest, she ran on, 'You could, you know, you've got plenty of pictures ready.'

For a moment an excited light broke over his thin features, then he said diffidently, 'I couldn't! I'm not ready. The family would give me hell about it!'

'Forget the family!' *Could you forget Brad?* Jacqui pushed the errant thought aside. 'There's no need to tell anyone else until the big moment. Look,' she leaned forward, her face animated, 'why not let me handle it and we'll have it all arranged in no time at all! It will have to be in no time at all,' she added, 'or it will be too late for me.' Why did she feel this pang at the thought of leaving? She forced her feelings aside. 'Listen, I'll get in touch with one of the picture galleries in Rotorua—lots of them exhibit the works of local artists. I'll arrange for the framing to be done in a hurry.' She smiled up at him. 'Well, what do you say?'

'Sounds tremendous,' all at once his face fell, 'but it might cost the earth. I mean, I couldn't hope to sell any of my work.'

She knew he was putting forward excuses. 'It won't cost all that much and you'll sell plenty! You might be surprised!' Something of her enthusiasm must have rubbed off on him, for he straightened drooping shoulders and stood tall, with a new look of confidence about him. 'It's worth a go, if you're sure you can cope with the arrange-ments——'

'I'm sure! I've been through it before, in London, with my artist room-mate.'

'Was it a success?'

'Not financially, but it was good experience and my friend got her name known.' She caught the despairing droop of his lips. 'But her work didn't compare with yours! Your pictures have got something special, different from any other artist, a depth and clarity somehow. Other people would see it too, if you gave them half a chance.'

'You're sure you won't mind the organisation bit?' She could see Chris was still unconvinced of his talents and seeking a way out of exhibiting his pictures.

'Mind! It will be something to do, keep me busy.' *Stop me from thinking of the boss all day long, hating him. Somehow I can't get him out of my mind.*

'Just in case anyone comes snooping around here.' She realised that Chris was throwing a cloth over the portrait.

She said thoughtfully, 'What you need is transport. The big old car out in the garage, is it yours?'

He nodded. 'All I need is somewhere to go!'

Jacqui flashed a smile in his direction. 'You've got it—partner!'

Back in the house there seemed no one about and she wasted no time in looking through the yellow pages of the telephone directory. Selecting an art room named The

Gallery, she rang through. Luck was with her, for the pleasant-voiced woman assistant answered, Yes, they could arrange for an exhibition of paintings in two weeks time. Could the pictures be sent in tomorrow so that details of framing and hanging could be arranged?

She couldn't wait to tell Chris about the booking, but when she hurried out to the shed there was no response to her knock, nor did he appear at the dinner table that evening.

'I suppose he's got one of his low moods again,' Aunt Tessa told Jacqui resignedly.

'But he's ever so much better,' Mrs Beeson put in with her bright smile, and removed his plate from the table.

When the meal was over, the men moved towards the billiards room and Bernice and Rick went out into the purple dusk of twilight. Jacqui helped Mrs Beeson to wash and dry the dinner dishes, then, unable to contain herself any longer, she hurried outside and ran through the orchard. A gleam of light was showing under the door of Chris's studio room, and hesitantly she gave a light tap on the door.

'Who is it?' a voice called.

'Me, Jacqui!'

'Oh, it's you. Come in!' Surrounded by paintings, he looked flushed and animated, a little too animated perhaps, she thought, but at least he was no longer depressed. 'I'm going through this lot, getting them ready for the showing.'

'Is that why you didn't come down to dinner tonight?'

'Dinner?' He stared at her vaguely. 'I never gave it a thought.'

Jacqui shook her head in mock disbelief. 'Mrs Beeson was sure you missed out because you were so miserable!'

He grinned. 'Too happy, actually! Look, I've sorted out all these and I've even managed to dig up a few old ones I painted ages ago. They don't look too bad, and the frames will make a heck of a difference.'

'That's what I've come to tell you.' She dropped down

on to the bed. 'It's good news. Everything's arranged for
your exhibition at The Gallery in Rotorua on the twenty-
eighth, that is if you can take the pictures in for framing
tomorrow.'

'Tomorrow? That doesn't give us much time.'

'Time enough. Let's get started. I'll help.'

'Good girl!'

They were a long time sorting out which paintings to
take, which to leave, cleaning the canvases and arranging
them according to size. Chris, who had seemed such a
quiet man, now seemed unable to stop the flow of talk as
he discussed the coming exhibition. Taking in his trans-
figured face, the excitement in his eyes, Jacqui told herself,
It's just got to be a success. If he fails at his, if he doesn't
sell anything, he'll never try again!

It was late when at last the canvases were finally stacked
into neat piles and the list of measurements for framing
written out. Jacqui stifled a yawn. 'It's been a long day.
You'll be getting away early in the morning, then?'

'Will I ever!' Two spots of colour burned in his cheeks.
'You won't see me for dust!'

'Okay then,' and she moved to open the door.

'And Jacqui——' She paused in the opening, eyeing
him enquiringly. 'Just—thanks a lot!'

'The good things haven't started yet! You wait!' She
blew him a kiss and turned away, to run full tilt into
Brad. What was he thinking about her and Chris? He was
with Sue, she realised a moment later. The two had come
from a late swim in the pool, taking a short cut through
the orchard. They must be, the thoughts ran wildly
through her mind, for even Brad surely wouldn't stoop to
check up on her movements. 'Goodnight,' she muttered,
and caught Sue's mocking laugh.

'Well, well,' the words came clearly on the still night
air, 'another secret assignation! You'll have to watch your
Miss Masters, Brad, she's quite a girl! First she has Rick
and even old Bill Lewis running around in circles finding
her a horse to ride—if you can call it riding, that is. Then

she stages a dramatic rescue out in the paddocks, now it's Chris she's working on! Before you know it, she'll be worming her way in here for good, one way or another!'

Jacqui didn't catch Brad's answer, only the low grated murmur of his voice. She had no need to hear the words; she could guess exactly what he would be saying and thinking. The temptation was almost overpowering to catch up with him and cry, 'Look, it's not like you think about Chris and me! Truly! You've got to believe me!' But that was Chris's secret and she had given her word. For Brad and the rest of the family to know of the coming exhibition of Chris's work would be to ruin everything. For somehow she knew that should the venture fail he would never summon up the get-up-and-go to try again.

Lost in her thoughts, she followed the other two up the winding path, unseeing of the moonlight that silvered the scene around her. She was unaware that she had come so close behind them until suddenly Sue's strong carrying tones reached her once again. 'Isn't she that guy Nick's sister? That family sure are bad news for our Chris! Oh well, I guess he can take care of himself, he'll need to with that one!' The next moment the two dark shadows ahead passed out of earshot.

Jacqui was so angry she felt herself trembling with the force of emotion. How dared she! How dared she say such things! And Brad, even though she hadn't heard his comments, hadn't he already lectured her in the matter of her friendship with his brother? Poor Chris, who so desperately needed her help. Oh, she hated them both! Brad and his girl-friend with her imperious ways and edged remarks. She never wanted to see either of them again!

A long time later as she lay in bed courting sleep, she heard the sound of Sue's car motor starting up for the long drive away from the station and back to her own home.

When Jacqui went out to the shed the next morning she found Chris seated despondently on the couch, his head in his hands. She had a dreadful suspicion that he had slipped back into his old state of depression, but she flashed a bright smile. 'What's wrong, aren't you feeling well?'

Avoiding her gaze, he shrugged indifferently, 'You could put it that way.'

'But you're going into town to take your paintings in to the Gallery?'

He said very low, 'I'm not taking them.' Then, in a rush of words, 'What's the use? They'll think I'm just a big joke, a guy like me who's never sold a thing in his life. I know that place The Gallery, it's where all the professionals exhibit, I've just remembered, the ones who've made it. Have you any idea of the price they put on their pictures? It's way out of the reach of the ordinary buyer. Now if you'd got in touch with a little coffee shop I'd have been all for it!'

'No, you wouldn't! You'd have got cold feet at the last minute just the same! Believe me, you're good! Just give yourself a chance! You'll be a great success——'

'So *you* say!' His lips twisted in a mocking grimace.

'No one else has ever had a chance to give an opinion of your work, you've never let them see it! Oh, come on, Chris,' she sat down at his side, rumpling his hair, 'snap out of it!'

'I'm not going!' he persisted stubbornly.

'I'll come with you and see the Gallery manager.' Jacqui was seeking desperately for some way she could change his mind and convince him that the effort was worthwhile. 'You won't have to do a thing about it except take me into town with the pictures and bring me back afterwards. Is it a deal?'

He grinned sheepishly, then said on a sigh, 'All right then, I'll give it a go! So long as no one around here knows anything about it.'

'They won't, until the right time. When they see those little red sale stickers they'll all be so proud of you——'

Chris gave a hollow laugh. 'That'll be the day! He added morosely, 'Brad will think I've really gone round the bend this time!'

'It doesn't matter what Brad thinks' she said firmly. The phrase was getting to be a habit with her, she told herself.

Could it be because she had to keep convincing herself that Brad's opinions were of no importance to her at all? She *had* to, because always deep down in her mind was the sneaky suspicion that if she gave herself a chance to know him, to believe in him—but it was out of the question because of Nick and her loyalty to him. If only—She wrenched the treacherous longings aside. Aloud she said, 'Look, I'll meet you in half an hour down in the garage. Think you can manage to get this lot,' she indicated the pile of paintings, 'into the car without anyone catching on?'

'Don't worry, I'll wait my chance.' Chris's tone was apathetic, but at least, she thought in relief, he hadn't refused to go into town. For a while it had been touch and go, but now she felt certain he was about to gain the recognition he richly deserved.

In her room she ran a pink lipstick over her lips and added a smudge of eye-shadow to her lids to complement the blue of her eyes. It was unfortunate, she mused, that everyone thought she looked so much younger than her years. Today she had to eradicate that mistaken impression. Her hair, swirled high on her head in a chignon, helped, as did the deceptively simple softly-clinging cream dress with its swirl of pleats in the skirt and dainty cream high-heeled shoes. 'That's the best I can do!' She slung her embossed leather bag over her shoulder and went down the hall.

In the dining room Bernice and her mother were eating a late breakfast. Bernice looked up enquiringly. 'How come you're all dressed up at this hour in the morning? Expecting someone interesting to turn up today? Are you keeping something from us?' she asked laughingly.

'You'd be surprised!' Jacqui perched on the edge of the table, then remembering that today she was supposed to look and act in a more responsible fashion she jumped down. 'Actually,' she said, 'I'm off to town!'

'That's nice, dear,' Aunt Tessa was buttering a slice of toast, 'you'll enjoy a day at the shops in Rotorua.'

'That's right.' Jacqui clutched wildly at the proffered excuse and wondered wildly whether Bernice would wish to accompany her.

It was however, Brad's deep resonant tones that came to her ears. He was standing in the doorway, thumbs hooked in the low-slung belt of his jeans, listening—just listening. 'If you're wanting a lift into town,' his gaze took in her elegant appearance, 'I'm taking the truck in today.'

'Lucky you!'

He went on as if she hadn't spoken. 'I've got to meet a guy in town and pick up a sheepdog from him. He's driving through from further up country.'

Her eyes sparkled with the anger he had roused in her. Did he lump her in with the sheepdog? Probably. Her soft lips tightened and she knew that now was her moment to take her revenge on him. For the memory of his and Sue's shared laughter in the pool outside on the same night that he had kissed her in the forbidden cave still rankled. But of course she didn't figure in his scheme of things, except maybe as a nuisance. Now was her chance to even the score, and she took advantage of it.

'Sorry,' somehow it was easier to draw herself up to her full five feet three, in her swirling creamy dress and slender high heels, 'but I've promised to go in with Chris.' There! That should show him that he had no monopoly on motor vehicles—or feminine companions!

'Chris?' He stared at her incredulously. 'He hasn't driven his car for months, not since——'

Jacqui lifted her small rounded chin. 'He will today, he promised!' The silence seemed to last for ever. Then, 'It's up to you,' he rapped, a contained anger in his eyes. Clearly it was a new experience for the boss to be turned down by a girl in favour of his younger brother. The thought ran through her mind that she should be delighted at gaining a victory over Brad, she was really, but on another level there was something about the long drive over the country roads *with him* that was wildly exciting and very hard to refuse. Even if they did spend the time quarrelling with each other, as they invariably did! The next moment she told herself that she must have dreamed up the shadow of disappointment that had clouded his eyes. Or had it been there it would be merely because for once in his life as king of the castle, he hadn't been able to arrange matters the way he wanted, to order her to comply with his wishes.

'I'd better get cracking.' He turned away, tossing over his shoulder to Jacqui as he passed, 'Might see you around town,' then he was gone.

Aunt Tessa gazed after him, a speculative gleam in her eyes. 'I might go along with him,' she mused, 'just for the ride.'

'I wouldn't if I were you, Mum,' Bernice advised dryly. 'Brad's got that look about him he gets when he's hopping mad inside and trying not show it. He goes sort of white around the mouth. When he's in that mood it pays to keep out of his way. He'll drive like fury, and you know what the roads are like on the way!'

'My goodness, yes!' Jacqui suspected that Bernice was playing on her mother's weakness, for evidently Aunt Tessa was a nervous passenger.

'Maybe you're right,' the older woman reached for another slice of toast. 'I don't think I'd really enjoy the drive with Brad in the mood he's in right now.'

CHAPTER SEVEN

' 'Bye now.' Jacqui lifted a hand in farewell and left the
room before she could be forced to parry any further
awkward questions. Hurrying down the steps, she told
herself that it was ridiculous for her to imagine that Brad's
ill humour stemmed from her refusal to take up his offer
to accompany him into town today. It must be some other
factor, an argument with one of the stockmen probably,
that had triggered off his dark mood.

What if Chris had changed his mind about the trip?
In the garage, however, she found him already seated at
the wheel of a big late-model car that was mud-caked and
dust-covered. He looked pale but determined, having evidently made up his mind to see the venture through.

'Hop in!' He leaned over to fling open the passenger
door. 'I was dead scared the battery might have had it,
the old bus has been off the road for quite a while, but it's
all right—listen! He pressed the starter motor and after a
moment's delay, the engine sprang to life to purr encouragingly. 'Hey,' his voice held a note of alarm, 'what
have you been saying to Brad? You haven't let on about
these,' he jerked his head to the pictures stacked in the
back seat, 'have you?'

'No, no, of course not. I told him I was going into town
with you, that's all. He did offer to take me——'

' "That's all," she says! He's just about berserk in that
quiet way of his!' Chris was guiding the car out of the
garage and they took the winding path leading to the
main road. 'He came down here and man, did he read
me the riot act! Told me he'd beat all hell out of me if I
dared to put my foot down on the accelerator. I gathered
that if I let anything happen to you I'd be torn limb from
limb! If I bought it today in a crash-up that was nothing,

but if *you* got hurt——' He swung her a puzzled look. 'If it had been Sue that all the fuss was about I could make some sense of it, but he never seemed all that interested in you——'

'He's not. He doesn't even like me.' It was true, so why did she feel a pang when she put the thought into words? She wrenched her mind back to Chris's bewildered tones.

'I don't know what's got into him.'

'I do. He offered to take me into town with him, but I said I was going with you.' She added dryly, 'He didn't seem very pleased.'

'So that was it!' She saw Chris's pale face relax. 'Guess it's not the reaction he's used to. Any other girl would have taken him up on it.'

'Not me,' Jacqui said firmly. 'We're in on this together, remember? You don't think I'd abandon our big project just to get a ride into town with Brad, do you?'

He sent her a quizzical look. 'Most girls would. You'd be surprised! They'd abandon anything else, and that includes the latest boy-friend, to go out with him. He's all right, but I can't see what they see in him myself.'

'Me neither,' agreed Jacqui, and couldn't avoid seeing the big black letters that had popped up in her mind. LIAR.

Chris thumbed the starter and they shot through the yards.

Three gates later they were turning into the winding metalled road with the hills rising all around them and the ranges fading to blue in the distance. Above them, ominous grey clouds were massing and presently a soft rain misted the windscreen. The ranges were a blurred no-colour silhouette on the horizon and a drifting white vapour veiled the thickly growing bush and tall trees around them.

Soon the rain became heavier, streaming down the windows and blotting out the dull glow of the sun in a leaden sky. Once they swung around a bend and Chris braked violently, just in time to avoid a drover who, with dogs and packhorse, was driving a straggling group of steers on the lonely highway. It took some time for Chris to manoeuvre the car through the heaving black bodies, then once again they were on a clear road. As they took the blind hairpin bends at breakneck speed Jacqui reflected ruefully that maybe Brad did have some justification for ordering his brother to drive more carefully.

Scenes appeared like magic out of the gloom—a fragment of roadway ahead, an outcrop of limestone rock on a steep hillside. The wind was rising now, sending tree-tops billowing. They had climbed so high on the slopes that she could feel on her face the moist breath of the clouds. It was a world bounded by the toa-toas, waving their bedraggled plumes at the roadside, and a fragment of highway lost in wet bush ahead. Once as they climbed towards the summit of a high hill, a railing loomed up out of the mist and she peered down, down, through shrouded tree tops to the road far below, shivering at the depth of the sheer drop. Then all at once the sun struggled through clouds, sparkling on tree-ferns and bushes and making the vegetation around them look newly washed. Like a stage curtain, the drifting haze fell away to reveal, far below, the grey-blue surface of a small jewel-like lake. She could see the tree-shadowed water by the shore and swishing white-caps on the wind-ruffled waters.

Peering forward to obtain a better view, she cried excitedly, 'Isn't that the little lake where Nick used to fish for trout?' She spoke unthinkingly. 'You know, when he was at Te Kainga?'

'Did he?' Chris's voice was off-putting. 'I wouldn't know.'

'So he told me.' Jacqui could have kicked herself for introducing the one name she should have kept quiet about. To change the subject she heard herself saying, 'Whereabouts is Sue's home? We haven't passed any other homesteads all this way.'

'You wouldn't. Her folk live in the other direction. Ten miles from our station, as the crow flies or the Land Rover travels. Although Sue seems to live permanently with us. Oh well, I suppose she will one of these days, so I may as well get used to having her around.'

Somehow the careless words fell on her heart like heavy stones. She forced her voice to a light note. 'Do you like her?'

Chris grinned. 'Not much. She's too organising for my taste. She's okay, so long as she's having everything all her own way, but try crossing her and wow, you're in for it! She's a bit like the furniture at home, she's been around the place for so long.'

Jacqui tried not to sound interested. 'How long?'

'Years and years, I've lost count. Everyone takes it for granted that she and Brad will get married one of these days. She was married once,' he ran on, 'but it didn't last long, just a matter of months, then they parted and she came back to the old home.' *And Brad!* The thought came unbidden, and brought with it a curious desolate ache to her heart. 'The story was,' his voice brought her out of her reverie, 'that he liked city life and she was all for the country. He was a quiet sort of guy and if you ask me, he got fed up with being organised. Anyway, they decided to call it a day. He went back to his stocks and shares and she promptly had her name changed back to what it was before she was married and took up breeding show jumpers instead of a family!'

'She's lovely to look at,' Jacqui mused wistfully. 'I would have thought that an artist like you would be really taken with Sue. I never saw a woman so beautiful——'

'Not to me!' Brakes screaming, Chris took a hairpin bend on the wet road at speed, scattering metal around the wheels. 'Sue's too perfect, too stereotyped. Know what I mean? That's the reason she carried off the national beauty contest a few years back. She was exactly the type the judges were looking for. Me, I go for something different in a girl—it's hard to explain. It's not always anything that hits you with the naked eye, but the moment you see it you know it's what you've been looking for and

you can't wait to get it down on canvas!' Once again
Jacqui was struck by the note of professionalism in his
tones. '*You've* got that certain something.'

'Me?' She was so surprised that the word came out as
an astonished squeak. 'What have *I* got?'

He flicked her a sideways grin, then his gaze returned
to the gleaming highway ahead. 'If you didn't see it for
yourself in the portrait I painted it's no use my trying to
spell it out.'

Hastily she said, 'Don't bother, I'll take your word for
it!' For no way would she admit that she knew only too
well the secret the portrait had unwittingly revealed—the
soft vulnerable bemused expression of a girl deeply in love,
even if she refused to admit it to herself.

She longed to ask Chris whether Lorraine had had for
him that mystique that so appealed to his artistic sense,
but something stopped her. He had not included the girl's
picture in the art work for the exhibition and she retained
only a vague impression of the portrait. In that fleeting
glimpse, Lorraine had appeared to be an ordinary enough
type of girl, but maybe Chris saw her differently. He was
in love with Lorraine, she reminded herself, and love came
quite regardless of appearances or anything else. There
was just no accoounting for it.

Chris, who had been silent and nervous at the start of
the journey, was now chatting happily as he discussed the
merits of the use of acrylic paint in pictures and the ad-
vantages of first capturing scenes by colour camera.

Presently Jacqui became aware that they were running
on a road cut through a vast sea of sombre pine plantations that covered the surrounding hillsides. Then after a
time they turned into a bitumen highway and at intervals
she caught sight of red-roofed farmhouses with their shel-
terbelts of native trees.

All at once they swung into a main road where the
country traffic, consisting of long silver milk tankers, log-
ging trucks and stock carriers, gave way to cars and tour
buses. On either side of the highway, trim suburban bunga-

lows painted in rainbow tints were set behind neatly
kept lawns with flower borders of vibrant shades. Then at
last they were approaching the tourist town of Rotorua
with its flowering trees and shrubs, its wide streets where
wisps of steam rose from fissures in the bitumen and house-
wives cooked their meals with underground steam. Borne
on the wind was the strange sultry odour that character-
ised this town that was the centre of one of the most spectacular thermal areas on earth.

Soon they were passing through the picturesque town
with its attractive timber motels and streets where store
windows displayed an endless assortment of summer mer-
chandise. Jacqui asked suddenly, 'Do you know the
address of The Gallery?'

'Do I? I've been looking in at exhibitions of paintings
there for years. I never thought that . . .' Chris's wistful
tones trailed away.

'Well, now's your chance!' Jacqui encouraged.

He threw her an uneasy glance. 'You reckon?'

She realised he was once more overcome by doubts as to
his ability to see the venture through today. Deliberately
she made her voice light and confident. 'I'm sure of it!'

At that moment he braked to a stop outside a wide
plate glass display window with its gold lettering, 'The
Gallery'. Inside a few paintings were on display.

Chris, however, made no effort to leave his seat. He sat
perfectly still, nervously biting a fingernail. 'This place
isn't for me.' His voice was low and distressed. 'I should
never have let you jack it up for me! Like I said, one of
the coffee lounges would have been more in my line. They
don't price the work high either. We should have gone
there!'

'No, we shouldn't!' Jacqui spoke with more confidence
than she felt but this was no time to be discouraging.
'Start at the top!' she told him with spirit. Any artist who
is given space here to exhibit his work is proving he's got
something worthwhile to sell, at the right price! Don't
you see?'

He brushed her words aside.

'We're wasting our time! They'll never even look at my daub. I just can't go barging in there and pestering them with my lot. I'd feel a damn fool!'

Already his hand had moved to the starter, but Jacqui was flinging open the passenger door. 'All right, then, I'll go in and see what they say. We do have an appointment, don't forget!'

She picked up the heavy parcel and pushed open the door of the gallery. Inside, a smiling middle-aged woman with an intelligent face came forward to greet her and soon Jacqui was laying on tables the various canvases she had brought with her.

'But these pictures are really impressive——' The woman's voice quickened. 'The artist has got something quite individual in his technique of painting light and water. You only come across that sort of unique treatment once in years.' She studied the signature on a lakeside scene. 'Christopher Kent. I haven't heard of him, but I'm sure we very soon will, and so will a lot of other folk in art circles. You'd be surprised,' she went on, 'how difficult it is to get hold of the works of a promising artist before he becomes famous, as this man undoubtedly will be. Once that happens, of course, his work is priced way beyond the reach of ordinary buyers. You'd like us to exhibit these as soon as possible, you mentioned over the phone?'

'Please.'

'It will be our pleasure. Oh, Hamish,' she was speaking to a short man with a trimmed black beard and lively dark eyes who had come from a back room to join her, 'take a look at these, will you? We've got a new artist who's really going to make a name for himself!' She turned towards Jacqui with a smile. 'Hamish is my brother.'

The bearded man was running an expert eye over the pictures. 'Hmm, definitely shows great promise.' He looked towards Jacqui. 'We'd like to meet the artist. He's your——'

'Just a friend,' Jacqui laughed in sheer exultation. 'I'm

acting as a sort of sponsor for Chris. Just wait until I tell him all about this! He's very modest about his painting.'

'They usually are, the ones who have ability.'

'I'll bring him in to see you.' She hurried out to the car.

'It's all right,' she told Chris quickly. 'They're delighted with the pictures. Honestly!' For he was staring at her in disbelief. 'They're waiting to meet you.'

Still he hesitated. 'I don't think——'

'Oh, Chris!' She tugged exasperatedly at his arm. 'Come *on*!' He went reluctantly with her into the room.

Jacqui let Chris do the talking. Astonishingly, now that he was dealing with people who spoke his own language of art and beauty he forgot his diffidence, his words tripping over one another in his eagerness to communicate with the smiling couple. Details as to framing and hanging were arranged and a date set for a showing of his work in ten days' time.

'That's it, then! We'll get along. See you on the Big Day!'

'Goodbye and good luck,' the art director said with a smile. 'Not that you'll need the luck! Your work speaks for itself!'

Chris's thin face wore a bemused expression as he went with Jacqui towards the door. 'Oh, just one thing,' he turned to say over his shoulder. 'No newspaper advertisements, please.'

The friendly woman looked nonplussed. 'But you'll need the advance publicity to let people know about the exhibition.'

Avoiding her eyes, he said stubbornly, 'I'll take my chances!'

'Just as well I thought of that,' he said to Jacqui as they stepped out into the blazing sunshine of the wide street. 'Rick would get a heck of a lot of fun out of reading that advertisement in the local paper.' His lips tightened, 'And so would Brad!'

'Maybe,' she said slowly, 'Brad would be more enthusiastic about it than you think. You never show any of the family your work, so you can't blame them for not know-ing——'

'Hey,' his face was still flushed from the interview, 'whose side are you on?'

'What do you think?' Let's have a stroll around the town!'

To be in Rotorua was a delight, she thought, or was it the sense of achievement that heightened her pleasure today? Made her appreciate the clean streets drenched in sunshine, the sparkling atmosphere of gala and holiday time that pervaded the high thermal area. Along the centre of the wide roadway, flax bushes flicked their long green spears in the light breeze and the pavement was thronged with tourists from other lands. The visitors eagerly scanned the attractively displayed souvenir shops with their Maori wood carvings, iridescent paua shell ornaments, sheepskin mats and greenstone jewellery. The women were clad in sun-frocks in summery shades, the men wore cool short-sleeved coloured shirts, work shorts and sandals. Could it be the high altitude, she wondered, that made the sky so softly blue, so near you felt you could almost touch it? Tour buses glided past on the way to thermal attractions of Fairy Springs where great trout could be fed by watchers and nearby Whakarewarewa with its boiling springs and geysers.

She paused at a souvenir shop, her eye caught by the display of Maori artifacts in the window. Here were all shades of greenstone, the nephrite jade carved into tradi-tional forms. A tiny grotesque figure of a *tiki*, a leaping swordfish, a miniature club.

She became aware of Chris's soft voice. 'I reckon today calls for a little memento.' When she made to protest he refused to listen. 'I owe you a lot. Come on inside.' She was still remonstrating with him when he took her hand in his and drew her inside the store. 'Choose something you'd like.'

'I don't want anything,' she said in a sibilant whisper.

'Well, I want to give it to you. How about this?' He was gazing down into a glass case, his attention riveted on an exquisitely carved greenstone *tiki* hanging from a silver chain.

'It's beautiful,' she breathed before she could stop to think. 'But I couldn't—the price——'

'That's nothing to do with you.'

'But it is!' Trust his artist eye, she thought, to light on the greenstone pendant that was more than likely the most expensive item in the store.

He took not the slightest notice of her protests. The stubborn look was back on his face and she knew it was useless to argue further. Besides, she had the sneaky feeling that she had fallen in love with the pendant and it was very difficult to argue against having it.

She brought her mind back to his eager tones. 'There's one condition, though——'

Shaking her head in resignation, she smiled up at him. 'And that is?'

All at once she was aware of the store attendant, a middle-aged man with twinkling eyes. He was taking the greenstone pendant from the glass case. 'Madam will wear the pendant?'

'That's it! Chris's face wore a huge grin. 'How did you guess?' He wrote out a cheque and handed it to the attendant. Then he lifted the silver chain over Jacqui's dark head and the jade figurine lay smoothly on her tanned throat. She touched the stone, feeling a sensuous pleasure in the smooth surface. Something in that smoothness made her say hesitantly, 'It isn't—it couldn't be a genuine Maori *tiki*?'

The attendant looked surprised. 'I thought you would know that by the price. They're very rare, of course, but this came into the hands of a friend of mine, a gift from the Maoris to his grandfather in the early days. He asked me to sell it for him.'

'Oh!' Jacqui was still feeling slightly dazed when they went out on to the street. She turned to Chris indignantly.

'You know you shouldn't have done that! The *tiki*'s an heirloom! Heaven only knows what you paid for it. And you scarcely know me!'

'Long enough.' He grinned. 'Don't worry, money isn't my problem. Anyway, it's a day for miracles, haven't you noticed?'

His pleasure in the gift was so apparent that she abandoned her protests. What was the use anyway, with the greenstone figurine nestling against her skin. Aloud she said, 'I'll be afraid to wear it, now I know its value.'

'No, you won't! That's the condition, remember?' She had never seen him in this mood of elation, his face glowing with an inner light. 'Maybe it will bring you luck, and that includes me. We're in this together—mate!'

'If you say so,' she laughed, and they turned into the wide entrance of Government Gardens, taking a path winding past pools with wild ducks and swans. The perfume of roses drifted on the air and wisps of steam rose from the grounds. In the picturesque old building, once a bath house, they wandered into rooms filled with paintings. Jacqui knew by the intent expression of Chris's face that he would happily spend hours here. She touched him on the shoulder. 'Look, do you mind if I take off and do a bit of shopping in town? You know, girls' stuff. You wouldn't be interested.'

'Fine with me.' He was scarcely listening, his attention taken up by the portrait of a Maori woman wearing the traditional *moko* design of curves and scrolls tattooed on cheeks and lips.

'I'll be back at the car park near The Gallery at five. How does that suit you?'

'Fine, just fine.' She knew he would happily stay here for the remainder of the day.

It was fun to explore the colourful streets, to mingle with the holiday crowds making their leisurely way along the footpaths, to listen to the variety of accents she caught as she passed by. More than one shopper, both male and female, turned their head for a second look at the lovely young girl in the silky cream dress, her only jewellery a swinging greenstone pendant at her throat. A girl who seemed oddly unaware of her fresh and youthful attraction.

Certainly Jacqui's thoughts were not for herself. She found herself wishing she had a family for whom she could buy gifts. It would be such fun to choose them, but there was only Nick and she didn't even know where he was living. But he would write to her, of course. Even Nick would write a letter when he *had* to! She wouldn't be surprised if there wasn't a letter with a Canadian postmark awaiting her at the cottage. For Nick would have no address when he wrote to her. She couldn't think why she hadn't thought of a letter awaiting her in the cottage before.

The feeling of satisfaction in the matter of Chris's paintings and the difference it would make to his whole life to find himself appreciated, to feel he had a future in his chosen work, stayed with her all afternoon. The hours fled by almost without her noticing the passage of time and in the end she had to hurry to reach the car park in time. Most of the shoppers' cars had already left the parking area, she saw from the next street, so she'd have no difficulty in locating Chris's dust-smeared Holden.

Or would she? For as she neared the area she could see no sign of the car. It was incredible—she stared around her—the car must be here . . . but no. Could she have mistaken one parking area for another? she wondered in sudden panic—but no, there was the big Woolworths sign on the corner of the street. Never mind, she chided herself in an effort to quell her rising apprehension, Chris was rather a dreamy person and she could well imagine him losing count of the time. After all, anyone could find themselves late for an appointment. But as the minutes dragged on she began to feel anxious.

'Looking for someone?' A dust-covered truck drew up beside her and she looked up to find Brad gazing down at her from the driver's seat. Her heart gave a great leap, then settled again.

'You!' She stared up at him stupidly. 'What are you doing here?'

He eyed her with his bland and disconcerting gaze. 'Picking up this and that.'

Of course. Hadn't he told her that he too was coming into town today. He'd been furious with her because she had turned down his invitation to accompany *him*, instead of Chris. Somehow she seemed to have a knack of arousing that explosive temper of his.

Aloud she told him, 'I'm just waiting for Chris. We arranged to meet here. He said he'd pick me up, then we'd head off for home.' Home! His home, not hers! There she went again. If only she didn't keep saying that word! Had Brad noticed the slip?

Apparently not. He had dropped down from the truck and was lounging against the door of the vehicle. He appeared smiling and perfectly at ease. So why did she get this feeling of a panther crouched ready to spring? She said with more confidence than she felt, 'He'll be along at any minute now.'

'He won't, you know.' She was aware that he was observing her narrowly.

'He's not coming?' she echoed in a puzzled tone. She didn't trust his mocking tone, for experience had taught her that this was Brad at his most deadly. 'Why not?' she demanded.

'I told him to get on his way, that's why! He didn't mind too much when I put it to him that I'd see you back safely—seemed to be in a bit of a daze, actually.' He shot her a quick glance. 'The town a bit too much for a hermit like him? Or was it you?'

She pretended ignorance. 'I don't know what you're getting at.' Underneath the words, her thoughts were racing in wild confusion. If only Brad understood the real reason for Chris's unusual high spirits! One thing was clear, she couldn't get back to the homestead without transport and she had no choice but to ride back with

Brad. He was taking a punishing revenge on her for her refusal this morning to accept his offer of a lift into town. Who would believe he could be so petty, a man like the boss?

She looked at him suspiciously. 'I guess,' she said slowly, 'that I haven't much option.'

His grin was maddening. 'I thought you'd see it my way!' He threw open the passenger door of the truck.

Suddenly Jacqui was too angry to speak to him and pulling herself as far away from him as possible on the long seat, she lapsed into what she hoped he would take as a dignified silence. Three minutes later she broke it herself with a surprised, 'But this isn't the way home!' Home? There she went again.

Brad flicked her a sideways grin. 'Just filling in time.'

She was puzzled. 'How do you mean?'

'The sheepdog I'm due to collect, remember?'

'Oh, the *dog*?' She had a vague recollection of his making mention of picking up a sheepdog today in Rotorua. 'Oh, that?'

'Amazing how difficult it is to pin anyone down to a time,' he was saying, 'when they're coming in from a distance. Jim left a message for me in the local garage that he's been delayed with a breakdown to his truck and can't make it before eleven tonight.'

'Eleven?'

'That's right.' He was guiding the vehicle into a long stream of traffic passing through the main street.

'Too bad,' she said sarcastically, then once again she forgot all about her vow of silence. 'But I still don't see why you couldn't have let Chris take me home. It's not as if——' she broke off in some confusion.

'It's not as if what, Jacqui?' he enquired softly.

She sent him a quick sideways glance, but his gaze was fixed on the moving traffic ahead. 'Nothing, nothing. It's just——' she decided to come right out with it, 'why did you?'

'Put it down to a sudden longing for some feminine

company, someone to talk to on the way back.'

'Talk to?' She eyed him suspiciously. 'We spend all the time fighting!'

'That's what makes it so interesting! Besides, there has been the odd moment when——'

Hurriedly she cut in, 'What could we possibly have to talk about?'

'We'll find something,' his voice was careless. 'How about a bite to eat? We've got to fill in time somehow and there are some quite good restaurants around the town. How about——'

Jacqui hunched a shoulder. 'I'm not hungry.'

He ignored her comment. 'If you haven't any special preferences, you'll have to trust my judgment, right?'

She shrugged. 'If you like.' All at once it seemed a long time since she had eaten and she was hungry—very. Not that she would ever admit it to Brad, that would be the last thing she would do.

He parked the truck outside on the street and they went in the wide doors and were shown over the carpeted foyer to a corner table by a window. Jacqui couldn't help but be aware of the glances from neighbouring tables towards Brad, with his erect, compelling good looks and the small dark girl who barely reached his shoulder. A girl whose heightened colour and stormy expression betrayed a recent disagreement with her escort.

The place was small and intimate with candles flickering on tables and pleasant background music. It was difficult to maintain an angry silence, she found, when her companion appeared entirely uninterested in her frame of mind. He was beckoning to the wine waiter and handing her the huge cardboard menu with its cover design of steaming geysers and Maori meeting-houses. Jacqui found it useful for hiding her face while she scanned the bill of fare.

'What's it to be?'

She hesitated, endeavouring to conceal her interest in the menu. If only she hadn't developed this awful hunger!

'Pineapple juice for me, please, and I'd like a seafood cocktail. No entree, but I'd like to try the local trout, seeing I don't often get a chance. And you,' for a moment she forgot all about hating the man, 'I know just what you'll order. A man-sized steak with all the trimmings!'

All at once he smiled, a *real* smile without the rancour. 'How did you guess?'

She laughed. 'I have been out to dinner a few times in the past. And I do happen to have a brother——' She broke off, appalled at her carelessness, for at the mention of Nick's name all the lighthearted happiness of the past few minutes fled from Brad's face.

'Oh yes, your brother Nick.' There was a contained anger in his tone. The uneasy silence lasted all the time the waiter took the order.

Brad poured wine into her goblet and she gazed at him over the rim of her glass, but it was no use, the mood was spoiled. Somehow when they were together, things always happened this way. For something to say she asked, 'What was it you wanted to see me about?'

He sent her an enigmatic glance. 'Later will do.'

She had a sudden presentiment of trouble, but her smile was as bright as usual, at least she hoped it looked that way. 'It's not my fault,' she told him heatedly, 'that you always believe the worst of me!'

His tone was bitingly soft. 'Did I say so?'

'No, but,' something deep inside her prompted her to hit back, 'you don't need to. Anyway,' she sipped her wine and flung him a defiant glance, 'I'm the one who should be feeling annoyed, making Chris go home without me——'

Brad's thick black brows rose quizzically. 'Aren't you annoyed? Somehow I got the idea——'

'Anyone would be!' She avoided his eyes. All at once she was finding it very difficult to sustain her argument beneath his cool amused gaze. Watch it, girl, she scolded herself, or before you know it, you'll find yourself like everyone else at Waiwhetu station deferring to the boss and thinking his word is law. The thought sparked her to exclaim indignantly, 'Making me wait around the town for hours just because of your old dog!'

His tone was deceptively mild. 'Do you mind?'

'Of course I mind!' she flung at him. 'Chris and I had a lot of things to go over together.'

He shrugged, putting down his wine glass. 'He'll keep.'

'That's the way you always talk about him,' she cried hotly, 'as if he didn't matter, as if he were just nobody! Just because he isn't all engrossed in sheep farming like the rest of your family and doesn't care about riding and hunting or any of the things you do, it doesn't mean that he——' a couple were shown to an adjoining table and she dropped her voice to a sibilant whisper, 'that he isn't good at other things. For all you know he might have hidden talents——'

For a second Brad's gaze lifted and she saw the anger blazing in his eyes. 'Like picking girl-friends?'

'Oh, *you*!' she burst out, 'so that's what's bugging you!' Two flags of colour burned in her cheeks. 'You think I'm deliberately setting out to entrap Chris. Well, it's not true. And even if it were——' her voice broke on the words.

He eyed her with his cool gaze. 'Oh, come on, Jacqui, you know the state of nerves he's been in lately. It would only take an emotional setback, the sort you could deliver without a second thought, to send him right over the edge.'

'If that's what you think of me——' She sprang to her feet, but a strong detaining hand shot out and he clasped her around her slim wrist.

'*Sit down!*' He forced her back in her chair. 'There's no sense in ruining the meal, you've got a long drive ahead of you.'

'*Your* meal, you mean!' Nevertheless she remained motionless, choking down the fury and staring angrily at the platter of succulent food the waiter had placed before her.

'Let's drop it,' rapped Brad. Never, she thought, had

she seen eyes so coldly disturbing.

The food looked delicious and attractively served, yet somehow Jacqui's appetite had vanished. Not so the boss, she mused crossly, who proceeded to enjoy his massive steak with lashings of oyster sauce.

Over coffee, they sat in silence as other couples around them left their tables to dance in the cleared space. Jacqui told herself that of course she would refuse should he ask her to dance. That was, *if she could make herself say the words.* She had to admit that in spite of the hostility he invariably aroused in her, there was something about him, a male virility that at close quarters she found well nigh irresistible, idiot that she was! The beguiling rhythm of a popular dance melody echoed then and the flickering candlelight threw strange shadows. Could it be her imagination that made the planes of his lean face look sharply defined, cold and unfeeling? She wrenched her gaze aside and stared determinedly towards the couples moving on the dance floor. But she had no control over her thoughts, she found. The man seated opposite her emanated an aura of masculine magnetism that was positively devastating, at least it was to her. She should be grateful to fate for showing her right at the start of their acquaintance, the type of man Brad really was. Oh, he might be awfully attractive to other women but with her of course it was different—or was it? She thrust the disturbing thoughts aside.

His vibrant tones broke into her thoughts. 'Shall we go?' Stupid to feel this sense of let-down because he hadn't asked her to dance. She was glad, wasn't she? Of course she was!

Outside the gathering dusk was painting shadows on the bush clad hills around them and the sky was a deep translucent blue.

'Where are we going now?' Jacqui enquired as she climbed up the high step of the truck and Brad closed the heavy door. He went around to the driver's seat and pulled his long length in at her side. 'Just down to the lake.' If only he'd smile when he talked to her, she thought wildly. 'The Maori Concert Party will be putting on a shown down at Ohinimutu—you haven't taken that in in your travels, have you?'

She shook her head. A belated sense of politeness made her add, 'But I guess you've been to lots of concerts down there already?'

He sent her an unreadable look. 'Not like this.'

Her soft lips tightened. What he meant was, not with *you*, not with a girl companion he couldn't stand the sight of! Well, that went for her too. The feeling was very mutual. The only reason he had brought her here tonight was so that he could lecture her about Chris. But she would have her revenge on him for that, she vowed silently. Just you wait ten days, Brad, and you'll feel very differently about your precious brother! Thinking about her triumph over him, even if she had to wait a few days, gave a definite lift to her spirits, she discovered.

CHAPTER EIGHT

THEY moved through the quiet streets, then turned to skirt the darkening waters of a great lake, empty now of the black swans that cruised among the waterweed by day. Nearby the little white timber church of Ohinimutu with its intricate Maori carvings was a pale blur in the gloom and on the water Jacqui caught the swish and slap of wavelets. All at once, in spite of problems and accusations and the hateful attitude of the man at her side, a sense of tranquillity stole over her.

Brad drew the vehicle to a stop outside the Maori Meeting House with its crossed overhead beams carved in traditional scrolls and curves and soon they were strolling up the wide steps.

In the timber hall they found seats on long wooden forms and Jacqui gazed around her, taking in the intricately carved panels decorating the Meeting House, each design of which served to pass on a legend or family history in a race that had no written language. She looked at the empty stage, then her gaze roved over the audience, most of whom appeared to be overseas tourists. Jacqui tried to guess from which country the different groups came. Anything to combat this feeling of awareness that took over whenever she was close to Brad. Even here in the hall, she could feel the nearness of him. Her gaze went to his hands, bronzed, well-shaped. Who would believe he performed such heavy tasks in his daily work? So many others in the big hall, yet she was aware only of him. All right then, she thought, admit that he has an overwhelming physical attraction for me. Its something I've never felt before with any man and that's why I'm finding it so hard to fight against, for fight I must. If only he doesn't guess at my feelings for him! She stole a glance towards

the strong masculine profile, taking in with a sense of
pleasure the soft dark hair and clear tanned skin.

He sent her an impersonal glance. 'We're bang on time,
they're starting!'

The next moment a young Maori man, smiling and
happy with the grace and good humour of his race, took
the stage. After welcoming the audience he went on to explain that tonight his entertainers would endeavour to show,
by dance and song, the story of the Maori race, their arrival in a new land in the far Pacific and a new way of life.

Then the stage curtains parted and groups of men and
women were on the stage, the men bare to the waist and
both men and women wearing the swinging flax skirts
dyed in the traditional red, white and black of the *taniko*
pattern. In their long dark hair the women wore a plaited
flax headband, the men a feather. Soon they dropped to
the floor and with paddles in their hands, with swaying
bodies and harmonious voices, gave an impression of the
intrepid sailors of long ago who had taken their great
prowed canoes across the vast distances of the South
Pacific ocean to find the new land of Aotearoa.

Other traditional dances followed—the *poi*, with its
rhythmic flick-flack as women holding tiny balls made of
flax tied on long strings, with a movement of the wrist
sent the balls moving in patterns in the air, the 'stick'
game and a dance that marked the flight of the rare white
heron, the 'bird of a single flight'.

The dreamy movements were followed by a Maori war
dance where painted warriors with fiercesome grimaces
and the brandishing of spears stamped and yelled and
leaped in a wild frenzy that had once been the prelude to
tribal warfare.

At the end of the programme audience and the concert
party performers joined in the haunting song of farewell
so familiar to New Zealanders.

'Now is the hour
For me to say goodbye;

Soon I'll be sailing far across the sea.
When I am gone will you
        Remember me?'

Jacqui blinked away the stupid tears that misted her
eyes. She was touched by the words of the haunting
melody in this Maori Meeting House at the lakeside, *with
Brad*. Soon it would all be a dream and she would be the
one who would be far away. There was so little time left.
Suddenly the thought was unbearable.

Outside a full moon sprinkled silver dazzle on the waters
and dimly she could see the white caps near the shore.

Brad helped her up the high step of the truck. 'I've got
to shoot around to the parking area to meet Jim——' the
town clock chimed eleven strokes, 'he should be just about
there by now.'

No romantic imaginings for him, she thought ruefully.
But of course he loathes me, and I feel the same way
about him. Well most of the time. There were times when
she didn't trust her emotions when it came to Brad, he
aroused in her such a tumult of mixed-up feelings!

They reached the car park to find a single vehicle waiting there, and the sheepdog was soon transferred to Brad's
truck. The two men chatted together for a short time,
then Brad climbed back beside Jacqui and soon they were
out on the main road.

She was glad of the long seat in the truck, where she
could slide into a corner as far away from Brad as possible.
That way it was easier for her to fight against that
treacherous sense of intimacy on the long drive through
the night. A night when moonlight silvered the hills
around them, a night for love. Why must she keep thinking about love? she asked herself distractedly, and slanted
a quick glance towards Brad's strong dark profile. Tonight
he seemed disinclined for talk, and that suited her fine.
She already understood the reason why he had sought her
company tonight. He had made it plain enough, goodness
knows!

As the miles fell away and they went far into the quiet hills her thoughts drifted. She must remember to ask Brad ... a letter ... at the cottage ... Her eyelids drooped and she had a sensation of delightful lassitude and utter content.

'Jacqui! On duty! Wake up!' Hazily she became aware of a masculine voice, aware too of an arm thrown around her shoulders, an arm that was now being gently drawn away.

'What? Where?' she murmured dazedly. 'I—I must have dozed off.' All at once she realised just where she had dozed off, close to Brad's chest, his arm thrown protectively around her shoulders. 'Oh my!' She jerked herself to an upright position. No use pretending she didn't know that she had nestled happily in his arms for most of the journey. What was more, she had enjoyed it. She recalled her sensation of utter content just before she drifted into sleep. Aloud she muttered a little selfconsciously, 'Hope I didn't interfere with your driving.'

She caught the white gleam of strong teeth against the bronzed face. 'No problem.'

'I suppose you're used to it.' Now why, she wondered dazedly, had that phrase sprung to her lips?

'Not with you! With you, Jacqui, I get the feeling you're trying to get as far away from me as possible. You *must* have been sleepy tonight. Either that or I've got the wrong idea?'

He would needle her now. Befuddled with sleep as she was, she couldn't come up with a suitable answer, but it didn't matter. She stumbled out to open a gate, waiting to close it behind the truck. By the time they drew in at the last gate she was wide awake, cursing herself for allowing herself to be so stupid as to fall asleep against Brad's chest and, worse, to enjoy the sensation! No doubt about it, her subconscious was really playing her tricks today!

To her surprise he drove to the garages instead of going up to the house. Switching off the engine, he turned to face her. 'Jacqui, there's something——' The stern disapproving note was back in his voice.

'Don't bother telling me!' she flung at him. 'I know what you're going to say. You've said it already. It's about Chris——'

He said very low, 'I wouldn't ask you if it weren't important.'

'Ask me what?' But she already knew the answer. 'Lay off my brother, or else? Is that it? Well, I won't! He likes me and I like him. He's sort of depending on me and I'm not going to let him down——'

'But you will,' he cut in. 'It's just a game to you,' he grated, 'someone to amuse yourself with while you're here. He could get badly hurt. I doubt if he could survive another let-down, the state he's in at the moment——'

'You're all wrong about Chris,' she broke in. 'He's not mad about me. He likes me, we're friends——'

'Do you really expect me to believe you?' His tone was cold and accusing. 'How about this?' He put up a hand to the greenstone *tiki* nestling at her throat. 'Chris got that for you today, didn't he?'

Wildly Jacqui searched her mind to parry his question, but she could find no way around the direct accusation. 'Yes, but,' the words tumbled breathlessly from her lips, 'you've no need to worry, it's not like you think!'

'Isn't it?' The sarcasm in his tone cut her to the heart and for a moment she was tempted to admit the truth. And ruin Chris's moment of triumph—at least she hoped it would be a triumph—when he trusted her to keep silent?

'Don't give me that, Jacqui!'

At the cold contempt in his tone she felt anger rise in her like a black cloud. 'If you feel that way about me, I'll go! Just give me a day or so to get a placed fixed up for my horse, then you won't need to put up with having me around. That's what you're wanting, isn't it?'

'No!' The harshness of his tone startled her. 'You'll stay right here where I can keep an eye on you——'

'Like rescuing poor old Chris tonight from my wicked wiles? Golly,' the angry words tumbled from her lips, 'you must think I've got that certain something, to be so worried on his account!'

His tone was so low she barely caught the muttered words. 'I didn't say you weren't attractive.'

'Oh,' swiftly she grabbed the advantage he had handed her, 'do you really think so?' Mockingly she added, 'And to think I never knew——'

'Shall I show you?' He caught her roughly to him, so close she could feel the hard man-feel of his chest. Impossible to struggle, his grip was like steel. The next moment his mouth closed on hers with hard pressure, then he released her so abruptly that she shook her head, trying to clear her senses. Well, she thought dazedly, she had had her third kiss, the one that mattered, a kiss of anger, revenge, punishment. She pulled herself together and before Brad could stop her she had opened the heavy door and leaped lightly down to the ground.

'You don't need to drive me up to the house!' Her heart was still thudding wildly and she was scarcely aware of what she was saying, or that she was stumbling over ruts in the ground, running, running over the dew-wet grass. *Don't think of Brad*. But the thoughts came unbidden. His kiss . . . a punishing gesture designed to show her that she couldn't flaunt his orders with impunity. That should she persist in her friendship with his brother, she could expect no mercy from him.

Even though she no longer had need to sit for her portrait, afternoons found Jacqui bound for the studio, her cool peasant skirt sweeping the long grass of the orchard as she strolled between the fruit-laden trees. Munching an apple or nibbling a ripe peach plucked from the tree, she would drop down on a couch watching Chris at his easel. Often they scarcely exchanged a dozen words as he worked on, his gaze narrowed with concentration as his brush-strokes moved over the canvas with a newly-found confidence.

Jacqui didn't mind how long she stayed in the studio-shed with Chris. She liked being here, and besides, why not admit that she took a perverse delight in continuing with her daily visits just in case Brad might be curious enough to check up on her movements? She couldn't *wait* for the day of the exhibition when she could score a victory over him!

She hadn't realised that others in the house might also be interested in the visits until after dinner that night. She and Bernice were kneeling on the lounge carpet going through the records when under cover of the strains of music issuing from the stereo, Bernice said speculatively. 'You like Chris, don't you?'

Jacqui, searching for a favourite orchestral number, was scarcely listening. 'Uh-huh! He's nice, talented too—Oh, here's the one I want! You'll be hearing his name a lot one of these days! Who knows, he might become famous!'

'But that's not the reason you see so much of him?' Bernice persisted enquiringly. 'You seem to prefer being with Chris to any of the other males around the place.'

Afraid that she might betray her secret, the disturbing attraction Brad had for her, *against all reason*, Jacqui said lightly, 'He's the only one who's free—well, in a way.'

'That's right.' Bernice gave up trying to draw Jacqui out on her love life. 'Brad's got Sue and Rick's got me,' worriedly she pushed the dark hair back from her fore-head, 'in a way. He doesn't dislike me,' she said wryly, 'he seems to like to have me around. He'd probably feel the same way about me if I were a boy, sort of matey, you know?'

Hands linked around her knees, Jacqui gave the matter some thought. 'What he needs is a shot of jealousy.' She smiled across at Bernice's wistful eyes. 'It just might wake him up to what a nice girl you are!'

'Fat chance!' Bernice pulled a face. 'Who's he got to be jealous of, even if I did follow your crazy advice?'

'When there's a *hangi* on here tomorrow night?' Jacqui raised expressive eyebrows. 'Chris tells me there aren't any invitations sent out because everyone for miles around comes anyway. And isn't there a dance in the woolshed afterwards? There must be some local talent?'

Bernice shook her head. 'Not for me. And even if there were I couldn't care less, not with Rick around. 'Her sweetly curved lips drooped and the big dark eyes were wistful. 'Stupid, isn't it! He doesn't even see me, not *me*. To him I'm just a silly nit who hangs around watching him, just hoping . . . just hoping.' She bit her thumb nervously. 'I shouldn't keep coming here for holidays. I know that it's asking for trouble, but somehow,' her voice broke, 'I always think that this time maybe. . . . Especially,' she went on after a moment, 'when he's "between girls" as he is now, if you know what I mean. And don't tell me to forget him,' she added fiercely, 'because I've been trying to do that for ages and it doesn't work! Guess I'm just that sort of girl. You know? The ones who get hurt again, and again, and again! The faithful kind! Sometimes I wish I were like you. You don't give a damn for any man, unless it's Chris——'

'Sorry,' Jacqui grinned, 'not that way!'

'You can even give Brad as good as he gives, and that takes some doing! Most girls are crazy about him!'

When Jacqui made no answer Bernice went on: 'There's this other guy at home. He likes me, *really* likes me, I mean. He teaches at the same school as I do and I know he'd do just about anything for me. I like him too, but not that way—I wish I did! Anyway, I guess Neil is getting tired of waiting around for me to make up my mind about marrying him. He's got an appointment teaching overseas that he's taking up in a couple of months' time and I promised him I'd let him know how I felt about getting married and going with him. I wouldn't hesitate,' she bit on her thumbnail, 'if it wasn't for this thing I've got about Rick.'

'Why don't you tell Rick?' asked Jacqui.

For a moment a light leaped into Bernice's eyes, then it faded. 'And risk making a fool of myself? No, I just couldn't, and anyway it wouldn't make any difference! To him I'm just a kid who's been hanging around at holiday times for years. No, this stay here is my last chance,' her voice dropped to a hopeless note, 'and for all the difference it's made to Rick, I might just as well not have come!'

'Don't give up yet,' Jacqui's voice was warm with sympathy, 'there must be something you could do! He seems so lighthearted, but I've got a feeling that underneath all that, he'd keep things to himself, especially how he feels about you. I still think a spot of competition might get him to betray his real feelings——'

'What real feelings?' Like I said, there's no one around here anyway, to be jealous of!'

'Why not invite your teacher friend, then?'

'No, I couldn't do that! I've got another two weeks and then I'll have to go back and give Neil his answer.'

'Anything can happen!' Jacqui's tone was encouraging. 'Even in two weeks!'

'For you, maybe!' Bernice said enviously. 'But you're different. You're the sort of girl who *makes* things happen! Me, I just wait around and hope—and much good it does me! All the men like you—Rick's always telling me how great he thinks you are!'

'Rick? He scarcely knows me!'

'And anyone can see you've made a new man out of Chris. Since you came here he's quite changed. Do you know, I heard him whistling this morning when he went to that old shed he calls his studio, and Mrs Beeson's complaining that she can't keep up with his appetite these days. And even Brad ... All the other girls that come here have tried to get around him, but you argue with him. You don't even seem to care that he's the big boss around here.'

'There's good reason for that!'

Bernice, however, had caught the low muttered words. 'How do you mean?'

'Nothing! Nothing!'

To Jacqui's relief, Bernice was back with her own problems. 'Even when Rick kisses me, its a brotherly—sorry, cousinly—sort of a kiss. The man doesn't see me, not really. Sorry to inflict my worries on you,' tears welled in the great brown eyes. 'Tell me, what would you do about Rick if you were me?'

Jacqui flashed a smile. 'Hit him over the head with a brick to make him wake up—or failing that, I'd wear something clinging and very feminine and different to the *hangi* the men are putting on tomorrow night. *Make* him notice you! I've got just the thing for you,' Jacqui was warming to her subject, 'a nifty little number that I brought back with me from London. I'd love to arrange your hair for you too—if you'd let me? Remember, it's all in a good cause!'

'Over to you!' A tremulous smile lighted Bernice's heart-shaped face.

At the end of the week's work in the heat of summer, it seemed that everyone on the station was more than ready to relax and enjoy themselves at the *hangi* meal at the homestead. The dance to follow was an event in the isolated district and it was taken for granted that everyone who could come would attend.

Early in the day Brad and Rick had dug deep pits in an enclosure sheltered from prevailing winds by tea-tree bushes, and when, hours later, the river stones they had placed in the pits were red-hot, they raked away the fire and put in containers filled with pork, lamb, and the sweet native kumera. Then wet sacks were placed on top and earth piled back in the earth ovens in readiness for the evening meal.

The two girls spent the afternoon tinting their finger and toe nails and washing their hair, then sitting out on the back steps while the sun dried the strands to a silky softness. Jacqui eyed Bernice's dark hair flowing around her shoulders. 'Wear your hair loose tonight,' she advised, not mentioning that Bernice's hair, swept severely back from a high forehead, did nothing for the small pointed face.

Later, in Jacqui's room, Bernice dropped down to the bed and Jacqui ran a comb down the long, naturally wavy hair. Wearing a swirling crimson muslin skirt that Jacqui produced for her, together with a white embroidered blouse, the other girl had a vivid charm that was new to her.

'Wait, one thing more!' Jacqui sorted through a cardboard box and brought out two golden hoops which she proceeded to fasten to Bernice's ears.

Bernice shook her head and the big hoops jangled. 'I feel like a gypsy!'

'I know.' Jacqui stood back to admire her handiwork. 'An exciting-looking one too!' The change was startling, she thought. Why hadn't she realised before that, freed from an unflattering hairstyle and uninspired garments, Bernice was an extremely attractive girl?

At the mirror Bernice was studying her reflection. 'You know something?' she said with a smile. 'I don't really mind being a gypsy——' she flung around to face Jacqui 'How about you? What are you going to wear?'

'I've got something.' Jacqui was jerking from the wardrobe an off-the-shoulder dress in stark white. 'It's not important for me. No one's going to be all that interested in what I look like!' She thrust aside a mental picture of Brad's cool, assessing glance. She pulled up the zipper and fastened around her neck the silver chain with its carved greenstone *tiki* that had been her reason for choosing the white dress that contrasted so effectively with the apricot tan of her skin.

'Not even Chris?'

'Oh, he won't notice!'

'No,' said Bernice thoughtfully, 'I guess when people are really in love, they don't!' It wasn't exactly what Jacqui had in mind, but she let it pass rather than try to explain away the real reason for the long hours that she and Chris spent together.

At last, fresh and attractive in their cool light dresses

and string sandals, they went towards the lounge room.
Lights blazed from open doors and windows and cars were
sweeping up the long driveway. Visitors were streaming
into the hall and it seemed to Jacqui that already the
main room was crowded with a laughing, chattering
throng. Aunt Tessa, her golden hair carefully arranged
and a cool caftan flowing around her ample curves, stood
in the open doorway welcoming the guests. Jacqui's gaze
went to Brad, whose tall figure seemed to tower above the
other men in the room. Gone tonight were his customary
open-necked cotton shirt and light work shorts and in their
place he wore a cream knit shirt and immaculately cut
fawn slacks. The unruly dark hair was slicked firmly into
its natural waves. The thought ran through her mind that
tonight he looked very much the master of Waiwhetu,
his manner at ease yet, in some indefinable way, carrying
authority. One couldn't help admiring him, she sighed—
anyone who didn't know him, that was! At that moment,
as if he became aware of her scrutiny, his gaze caught
hers and something flashed between them, then the crowd
surged between them, obscuring her vision.

As the two girls pushed their way through the throng,
it seemed to Jacqui that they were among a variety of
people—stock agents, sheep and cattle farmers, college
students at home for the long summer holidays, country
travellers, even, judging by the various accents she
caught, a smattering of overseas visitors. When Brad put
on a *hangi* and woolshed dance it seemed that all were
welcome at Waiwhetu. She recalled his unreadable
glance of a few minutes ago. Why must she be the one
person for miles who wasn't? Was that the wordless message he had signalled to her?

Aunt Tessa and the housekeeper were moving around
the room, greeting new arrivals and laughing and talking.
No one seemed to bother with introductions, there would
have been too many guests anyway, Jacqui mused.

All at once she became aware that two youths employed
as cattlehands on the station were making their way to-

wards her and Bernice. With their clean scrubbed faces and plastered-down hair, Jacqui suspected that both Terry and Tim would feel more at home on horseback than at a dance, even a woolshed one.

As they reached the two girls, the youths' friendly open faces were filled with a shy appreciation. 'Gee, we couldn't make out whether it was you two or not. We had an argument over it.'

'You mean,' said Jacqui with a smile, 'that you took a bet on it?'

'That's right,' Tim admitted. 'We were fairly certain about you, but Bernice,' he shook his head in mock amazement, 'we just didn't know she could look like this.'

'Didn't you now?' Bernice, as a rule so quiet and retiring, had a quirky smile and her eyes sparkled mischievously. Something of the brilliance of her costume seemed to have rubbed off on her, Jacqui thought. 'Cross my palm with silver, kind sirs, and I'll tell you your fortune!'

Terry said, grinning, but somehow meaning it, Jacqui thought, 'Just save me a dance, that's all!'

'Me too!' His mate took quick advantage of his opportunity. 'How about you, Jacqui?'

'If you like.'

The girls had seen the young stockmen riding over the paddocks and down in the yards dipping, but they lived in the single men's quarters and tonight was the first time they had spoken at any length together. As if determined not to let the girls slip away, Tim and Terry kept close by them and presently the group went with the crowd of people who were moving down the verandah steps and strolling through the rose-scented dusk towards trestle tables set out on the dried grass. Fairy lights had been strung in the trees overhead and on the tables were carafes of wine, glasses and cans of beer. Mrs Beeson had prepared great pottery bowls of salads of various kinds and small baskets of woven flax lined with snowy napkins, were set out in readiness for the delectable *hangi* food.

In the gathering dusk, the groups moved between the

tables and talk and laughter rose on the night air. All at once Jacqui became aware of Chris, who was threading his way through the groups in her direction. Evidently he came from the studio, for his hair was standing on end where he had run his fingers through it and he wore his customary paint-smeared jeans and T-shirt. 'Didn't know it was so late,' he came to stand by Jacqui and swiftly Tim pressed closer to her on the opposite side. It was all fun, she mused, and to a true New Zealander there was nothing to equal the succulence of food cooked in the earth ovens.

At that moment, through a gap in the throng, she caught sight of Brad and Sue, their heads close together as they shared some private joke. She was laughing up at him, the fitful gleam of a hanging lantern highlighting her blonde hair and throwing into relief the planes of Brad's face. Just a glimpse, so why did all the fun and lightheartedly gaiety of the moment fade away?

'Hey, Bernice!' Rick was bearing down on them through the shadows. 'I couldn't find you any place, thought you'd given it all away and were still up at the house—Wow!' The matey inflection of his tones gave way to a note of wonder. 'I never saw you looking like that before!'

Bernice sent Jacqui a wink. 'Jacqui's been working on me ... new hair-do, this gypsy dress with all the trappings——'

'You're a witch!' There was a new tone in his voice. 'And I thought you were just a cousin of mine!'

Bernice laughed. 'Second cousin, remember?'

'Yeah, yeah. For once Rick seemed at a loss for words.

Terry, realising he wasn't alone in his preference towards the exciting-looking girl at his side, said gruffly, 'Tim and me, we've got ourselves partners for the dance over in the woolshed,' and moved a fraction closer to Bernice.

There was a new decisive note in Rick's voice. 'I wouldn't bet on it. Why don't you go find yourself someone else?' he suggested, an edge to his voice. 'The place is full of strangers!'

'Who wants a strange girl,' Terry's boyish mouth was set in an obstinate line, 'when Bernice is right here?'

Jacqui took in the conversation with only half her mind. The other half kept reverting to Brad and Sue. At least she had a male escort tonight who would see she wasn't lacking a dance partner. She couldn't bear it if Brad, impelled by some feeling of duty, should ask her to dance, and she had no excuse for refusing him. For refuse him she would. She had this driving compulsion to hit back at him in revenge for the high-handed way he had treated her. Forcing her to stay in town hours longer than she needed, making her drive all the way back with him! All just to prove to her that he meant what he said when he'd warned her against any deep involvement with Chris. He would do anything, that man, to prevent Chris falling in love with her, as he mistakenly imagined had happened!

The stars were blazing in a softly dark night sky when at last the meal was over and cars and trucks started off for the short run down to the woolshed. Jacqui and Chris got into Chris's car and the others piled in. Soon they were climbing the steps to the lighted shed, where those who weren't dancing to the foot-tapping rhythm were seated on hay bales scattered around the big room. The ferns and flax the men had brought in from the bush earlier in the day, softened the stark outlines of the woolshed, the big tables recently in use by the shearers were scrubbed clean and the floor was slippery from the grease of a thousand fleeces.

Soon Jacqui was on the dance floor, Tim's face red with embarrassment as he attempted to follow the movements. 'Don't worry,' she sent him an encouraging smile, 'you'll pick it up in no time!'

Under the naked electric bulbs hanging overhead, couples moved and swayed around them. It seemed to Jacqui that everyone in the room was dancing. Well, not quite everyone, for out of a corner of her eye she caught sight of a group of men standing near the entrance. Brad, she would know his tall figure anywhere, was watching the scintillating scene, his gaze moving over the dancers as if searching for someone. At that moment Sue hurried to join him, tugging at his arm and pulling him with her on to the dance floor. How could Brad, Jacqui wondered, who was in charge of all this, allow himself to be influenced so easily by Sue? But of course, the explanation came unbidden, *wasn't it because he wanted to?*

When the number came to a close and couples were standing motionless on the floor she noticed Bernice, standing nearby with her young partner. The other girl looked flushed and animated. The next moment the orchestra picked up guitars and banjo once again and Bernice was whirled away by Terry. Rick, Jacqui noticed as she flashed past him, still stood on the fringe of dancers, a sullen, unhappy look on his usually cheerful face. So it's working, she thought, it's really working, the gypsy magic! For Bernice, admired and noticed by Rick, had an electric excitement about her in place of her moody hopelessness. Animated and laughing up at her partner, her long dark hair swung around her face as she moved to the rhythm of a hit tune that Jacqui had last danced to in faraway London.

Yes, it was Bernice's night, Jacqui told herself with some satisfaction. The other girl, like herself, was in constant demand on the dance floor, and all the time Rick continued to stand on the fringe of moving couples, a dark expression on his face. Only at long intervals did he manage to partner Bernice. Most of the time she was swiftly whirled away by Terry, who clearly saw no reason why he should not monopolise Bernice's time tonight. For once, Jacqui told herself, the ball was in the other girl's court. If only Bernice could be smart enough not to bungle her shots. So far she was doing fine—good for her!

All the time Jacqui had her own problems, or rather one problem, one man. Throughout the evening Brad hadn't approached her. Not that she expected him to dance with her, in view of their stormy moments whenever they found themselves together, and yet ... The dancing went on into the early hours of the morning and the strains of music for the last dance were stealing through the shed when she caught sight of Brad's tall figure advancing purposefully towards her. Her heart began to thud ridiculously. The next moment he had reached her side. 'Mine, I think?'

All at once she was seized by an instinct to escape, to take her revenge; she didn't know which, she only knew that in blind panic she turned aside and grabbed at Tim's hand—thank heaven he was close by—and they merged into the moving throng. A quick glance backwards showed her that Brad was standing where she had left him, his face cold and impassive. She knew so well the tightening of the lips that was one of the signs that she had really got under his skin.

So why did she feel no sense of triumph? She'd waited all night for the opportunity fate had handed her, to get her own back on Brad. Yet she felt no elation, only a chill, like a knife passing down, down through her body. Her limbs performed the familiar movements in time with the melody, but the feeling of let-down persisted and suddenly she was weary. Something of her feelings must have shown in her face, for Tim was saying hesitantly, 'My fault. I guess I've trampled all over your feet tonight!'

'Don't you believe it!' She roused herself to say encouragingly, 'My feet are fine, and you don't need to worry about your dancing any more!'

'It's been great, hasn't it, all of it?' Beads of perspiration shone on his red forehead and he looked pleased and happy.

Jacqui nodded. 'Quite a night!'

To her it seemed an age before the music crashed to a close and soon everyone began drifting towards the open doors and out into the open air.

Tim and Terry escorted the girls to the car where Chris

was waiting to take them back to the homestead.

'I'll see you again soon?' Terry was gazing adoringly towards Bernice, his warm tones low and pleading. 'Very soon?'

'You'll be lucky!' came a deep angry voice as Rick threw a masterful arm around Bernice's slim waist. 'Come on, you're coming with me!'

Terry's jaw dropped. His face darkened and for a moment Jacqui feared that Bernice would find a fight on her hands. That would be just a little too much in the way of masculine attention! The next minute, however, Terry, with a defeated hunch of his shoulders, turned away. 'See you around, Bernice!'

Jacqui got into the car beside Chris. It didn't help that at that moment Brad and Sue passed close by the car, and this time it was Brad's turn to ignore Jacqui's presence.

CHAPTER NINE

STREAKS of pink and gold stained the eastern horizon as the car drove up to the house. In the kitchen Mrs Beeson was preparing breakfast for the men. Because Jacqui felt too restless to go to bed now, she busied herself with clearing away the remains of the *hangi* meal, washing out salad bowls and running fresh water over glasses.

'You don't need to do that,' the housekeeper smiled, 'I'm used to it!'

Jacqui said, 'But I want to.' Oddly, it was the truth. She was glad of any activity that might dull the ache she couldn't seem to banish from her mind. Why didn't she feel happy and triumphant? This was what she'd wanted, wasn't it? To take her revenge on Brad for all the trouble he'd caused Nick and herself? She squirted detergent into the dishwater with an angry gesture. So why was she feeling angry with *herself*? Why must she remember, now of all times, the things about Brad that couldn't be faulted? A vicious shake of the detergent bottle sent bubbles flying in all directions. Why call to mind those fleeting moments that were unforgettable, his kiss in the cave, the times when he had seemed to forget that she was Nick's sister?

She was still busy in the kitchen when Bernice drifted in, her eyes soft and happy, her expression the look of a girl who had been well and thoroughly kissed, by the right man in her life.

Absently Bernice picked up a tea towel and began to dry a glass goblet. 'Enjoy yourself last night?'

'It was fantastic!' Jacqui hoped that Bernice in her present state of newly-found happiness, was too wrapped up in her own affairs to notice the forced note of enthusiasm in her tone.

'Brad didn't dance much, except with Sue. She seems to regard him as her own private property.'

A stab of pain shot through Jacqui and to change the subject she said brightly, 'You were the one all the guys wanted to dance with, especially Rick!'

Bernice sent her a wink. 'I only want one!' Her dark eyes sparkled. 'It worked, it really worked, that spot of jealousy you advised!' She moved to face a side mirror and put a hand to her flowing hair. 'Rick says he likes me to wear my hair this way.' She spun around. 'You know something? I thought I understood him so well, yet I never knew he had that jealous streak in his nature.'

'You shouldn't have let him take you so much for granted.'

'What could I do? That "cousin" idea put him off for a start.'

'And now?' asked Jacqui.

Bernice's smile held a hint of mischief. 'Now I can have things a bit my way. He's beginning to notice me as a real live girl! It's not much in a way, but it will do for starters—may I borrow your gypsy outfit again if he starts to slip back?'

'It's yours. I don't want it back, truly. It really does something for you.'

'Brought me luck for a start!' Bernice was too taken up with her own affairs to notice that Jacqui was reticent about her partners at the woolshed dance. 'I'm off to the shed to clear up the place, make it look like a shearing shed again—want to come? I couldn't sleep now anyway, I'm too excited!'

'Me too.' But Jacqui knew that her emotions were of an entirely different nature.

It was later, when she was carrying brushes and oint-ments up the hill, that she ran into Brad, on his way down from seeing to the chestnut foal.

Wondering how he would react to the slight she had given him last night, she sent him an uncertain smile, but his contained expression gave nothing away. A bare inclination of his dark head and he had gone on down the slope. Only the memory of his eyes, cold and angry, stayed with her.

To thrust away the memory of his hard stare, she busied herself with Pancho, tending the wounds that were healing rapidly now and brushing his coat. Definitely the horse had lost his shrunken appearance and was starting to put on weight. 'You'd better watch it, mate,' she told him, brushing out the long tail. 'At the rate you're putting it on you'll be ending up on a diet!' It must be tiredness, she thought dully, for even up here with Pancho, busy with tasks that usually absorbed her, she couldn't keep her thoughts from straying. It was that flint-like expression in Brad's eyes, she couldn't get it out of her mind.

The next day she wandered down to the studio shed to find Chris painting at his easel. 'Hi, Jacqui.' He tossed the words over his shoulder and she realised that he was concentrating on his work and clearly in no mood for company. Crossing the room, she came to look at the picture he was working on, a forest scene where a narrow bush track was lost amidst clustering tree ferns and the towering kauri trees that soared into the blue. Surely he hadn't hitherto worked with such speed and precision? Utterly absorbed in his task, Chris seemed scarcely aware of her, and after a time she softly closed the door and went away.

If only Nick would get in touch with her! Maybe if she put a call through to the lawyer once again, there just might be a letter awaiting her. She couldn't wait to find out and hurrying through the orchard she ran into the house. Luck was with her, because there seemed no one about. She put the call through to town and the lawyer answered her personally; she recognised his pleasant tones.

'You're still in Rotorua, Jacqui?'

'Just for a little while longer.' Why did the words bring with them a pang? 'I'll send you my new address when I move away.'

'I'd appreciate that. If it's about Nick you're ringing me, I haven't heard from him, but I'll contact you as soon as I do. You're at——'

'Waiwhetu station. It's in the back country of Rotorua district.'

'That's good enough for me. Look after yourself, my dear, and if there's any way I can help you, you've only to ask.'

'I know, I know.' The fatherly tone warmed her heart, but nothing could dispel the sense of disappointment.

'Bad news, I take it?'

She flung around to meet Brad's mocking glance.

'You heard?'

'Actually,' he said, an edge to his drawling voice, 'I'm waiting to use the phone.'

'Oh . . . sorry.'

'It's all right.' He made no move towards the telephone but continued to lean against the wall, and despite his easy stance she saw that his eyes were alert and watchful.

'It's just,' he might as well know, he knew already, didn't he, 'I was hoping to get some news of Nick, a letter maybe.'

His well-shaped lips twisted derisively. 'What could you expect him to write to you, in the circumstances?' he queried softly. 'Sorry, Sis, had to make a run for it when things got too hot around Te Kainga. Better luck next time! Something like that, hmm?'

'No!' She caught her bottom lip in her teeth. 'He will write, you'll see!' At the disbelief in his eyes she cried wildly, 'And when he does let me into what's been happening around here, you'll be the first to know!'

'Thanks very much.' His tone was laced with irony.

Suddenly a thought flashed into her mind and almost without realising it she was speaking her thoughts aloud. 'There just might be a letter from Nick waiting for me at the cottage. It might have come after I left there.' Her eyes were alight. 'There was a mailbox up the road. I didn't think of it the day we were at the cottage——'

Brad smiled his formidable smile. 'I did. And I've got the boys to check since. I don't know why, it's hardly likely——'

'Oh!' Jacqui's soft lips drooped. The next moment she raised clear blue eyes to his forbidding face. 'But he could still have written to me.'

'You reckon? Look here, Jacqui, if it makes you feel any happier I'm riding over to Te Kainga tomorrow to check on some stock up in the bush farm. There's a short cut over the hills and if you like——'

'No,' she broke in, 'I want to go myself.' Through her mind had flashed a picture of faded newspapers blowing around the roadside and under overhanging trees at Te Kainga. There was just a chance that Nick's letter was blowing around among the bushes too. Wouldn't it be worth anything to see for herself, even humbling herself to ask a favour of Brad?

She became aware of his scowling expression. 'Good grief, don't you trust me?'

'I just want to come myself,' she persisted stubbornly.

'You'd be going on a wild goose chase——'

'That's what *you* think!'

'Just tell me the way, then,' all at once she was feeling excited at the prospect. 'I can ride, you know.' At his satirical glance the colour flamed in her face, but she wasn't giving up yet. 'I really am experienced.' She added hotly, 'Whether you believe me or not! Which way would I go?'

'You'd never find those old Maori trails over the hills and through the gullies. And even if by some miracle you made it to Te Kainga, you'd be knocked out. It's a tough ride for a girl.'

'Doesn't Sue ever come with you on those trips?' The moment the words left her lips she regretted them.

'That's different.'

Her eyes were bright with defiance and anger. 'I'll come with *you* then! If you're shifting any stock,' she added eagerly, 'I could help you.'

'I scarcely think that will be necessary.'

But Jacqui refused to be defeated so easily. 'I'll just come along then for the ride!'

'No, you won't!' Brad told her fiercely. 'Because you won't get the chance. The last time you went for a ride I had to do a big rescue act——'

She flushed hotly. 'You won't this time! Just lend me one of the horses and I'll——' His look was so daunting that she broke off, remembering at that moment the dance last night and the snub she had given him in public, something he evidently hadn't forgotten. 'You won't know I'm there,' she finished.

'That's what I'm worried about, you'd be lying under a bush!' He gazed down at her eager young face and it seemed to Jacqui that the taut lines around his mouth relaxed a little. 'Forget it,' he said in a milder tone. 'I'll be away hours before you're even awake. You'd never make it.'

'Let me try!'

'Not a chance! If it's the letter that's on your mind, like I said, you'd be wasting your time, but I'll check, just to make sure——'

She said very low, 'And prove to me you happen to be right, as usual?' She couldn't resist the jibe.

'I am right!'

Oh, he was hateful, hateful! Choking down the tide of anger that threatened to overspill, she made one last appeal to his good nature. She despised herself for the appealing softness of her tones. '*Please*, Brad.'

'And don't waste your time trying out your feminine wiles on me,' he rasped. 'You won't find me such an easy mark as my brother.'

Jacqui gasped. 'If you only knew——' she began.

'Spare me the details,' he cut in with brutal frankness. 'I've got eyes in my head. Don't try to pull the wool over my eyes, because it won't work!'

'You——' Had there been anything to hand she could hurl at the dark mocking face she wouldn't have been able to stop herself from aiming it in his direction. As it was she found she was trembling. The shame-making thing was that she had let herself in for this. She might have known that he would take full advantage of such an opportunity. Blue eyes stormy, she held out the receiver. 'I thought you wanted to use the telephone,' she said coldly and pointedly.

'There's no hurry.' He appeared to have got his temper under control. 'I'll be back late tomorrow afternoon. I'll let you know then how I got on.'

'Don't trouble yourself.' Their glances clashed and held, then Jacqui was forced to drop her gaze. 'I'll find out for myself.' And that, she thought, as she lifted her rounded chin and marched determinedly from the room, will give him something to think about! As she ran down the verandah steps, plans rushed wildly through her mind. Brad would find that he couldn't so easily dispose of her company on his trip to the bush farm tomorrow. I'll get Rick to show me the way, she decided. No, not Rick with his practical jokes. He'd think it was real fun to get me lost up there in the hills.

Chris, then. He might take me if I asked him, but he's so deeply involved with his painting. The appreciation of the art gallery director has acted to him like a shot in the arm. Now he can't find enough daylight hours to do all he wants to. I can't ask him.

I know what I'll do. I'll go with Brad, and if he doesn't want me along I'll ride behind. I'll be such a pest to him he'll get fed up with trying to send me home and have to put up with me. It will be worth it all to get there and maybe find Nick's letter. Then I could really prove to Brad how wrong he was . . . all those lies he told me.

It was childish and absurd, but just at this moment what she wanted most of all was to prove to Brad that he knew nothing of her riding prowess, just as he knew nothing of Nick's real character. It must surely be his all-powerful position in this isolated area that gave him the power of making snap judgments. It was time someone showed him just how mistaken he could be!

The sight of a stocky figure down in the stockyards made up her mind and she hurried towards Bill Lewis.

He was crossing the yard when she caught up with him. 'You're just the man I want to see! I'm going for a ride early tomorrow morning and I wondered ... could you lend me one of your mounts? It doesn't matter about speed, just something dependable.'

He caught on at once. 'You want Prince. He's solid and strong and can go on for ever, the best stockhorse on the station. I'll put him in the yards tonight and he'll be ready for you first thing in the morning. You don't know what it's like here until you see the place at sunrise.'

'That's what I think too.' All at once Jacqui realised he was a man she could take into her confidence, quietly spoken, reticent with a weathered lined face and kindly blue eyes. 'There's somewhere I'd like to go tomorrow. It's the run-off at Te Kainga. Did you know my brother Nick? He leased it a while ago.'

'Heard he was there, never met him myself.' Jacqui felt inclined to believe that he knew nothing of the monstrous lies Brad had told her about Nick. The thought spurred her to say eagerly, 'I've heard there's a short cut over the hills. Do you think you could draw me a plan of the route?'

'Don't know about that.' Thoughtfully Bill scratched his head. 'Difficult to show anyone on paper. You really need someone with you.'

'Yes,' she said slowly, 'that's what I thought.' To herself she added. That's it, then. You're going to be stuck with me, Brad, *whether you want me or not!*

'There's one thing, though,' he murmured hesitantly. 'About Prince——' Was he recalling her earlier ride that had turned into a disaster? 'Reckon you can handle him?'

'Of course I can!' she assured him. 'What happened the other day when I went riding was just pure bad luck, that old girth and all.'

Still the stockman looked doubtful. 'Have you had a word with Brad about this little trip of yours?'

'Oh, he won't mind!' A dimple flickered at the corner of her mouth. 'He's coming with me.' Even if he doesn't know it yet, she told herself, and crossed her fingers in the hope that Bill wouldn't mention the matter to the boss.

She saw the leathery features relax. 'That's all right, then. I'll have him ready for you in the stables.'

'It's a bit early—five o'clock.'

'Not to me, lass.'

'Oh, *thank* you!' Such a tide of relief flooded her that she raised herself on tiptoe and brushed the leathery brown cheek with a fleeting kiss.

'Hey,' he looked pleased and surprised, 'what's that for? I haven't done a thing.'

'It means a lot to me!'

A smile tugged at his lips. 'Reckon for that I'd bring old Prince around for you every day of the week!'

She flashed a smile in his direction. 'Once will do for starters!'

Jacqui had no need of her little gold alarm clock, for long before the set time she was up and dressed in worn jeans and a cool open-throated white blouse. She didn't dare risk going into the kitchen to make an early morning cup of coffee, for fear of running into Brad there, but she had stuffed apples into her pockets.

When she opened her door to peer along the passage she could hear no signs of activity in the kitchen, but just to be sure she made her way quietly up the carpeted hall and slipped silently out of the door into a pre-dawn world. A breeze stirred the trees and a few faint stars still dusted the sky.

In the stables she found her mount, a massive bay horse of solid build. Definitely Prince wasn't a flighty type, at least Brad need have no worry on that score. After today's jaunt to the run-off Brad would have to admit that she was indeed an experienced rider. Brad. For some reason just the thought of him sent her tense and trembling so that her hands shook as she fitted the bridle, threw the blanket and saddle over the broad back.

By the time she had got her mount saddled and opened the stable door, a faint glow of sunrise stained the eastern horizon. She rode out into a world that was fresh and hushed and exciting.

She had only just gained the shelter of the garages when Brad emerged from the house and went to let the dogs off their chains in the kennels. Presently his long easy stride took him up the hill track and before long he was back, leading his big black stallion. When he had saddled his mount the sky was a palette splashed with the vivid flames and orange tints of a spectacular sunrise.

He was riding past the garages when Jacqui emerged from the doorway to pull rein in his path. At last, she knew, she had cracked his cool composure. 'What the hell,' he blazed, 'are you doing here?'

She nerved herself to sustain his accusing stare. 'Just waiting for you.'

She saw his lips tighten. 'I thought,' he said with harsh deliberation, 'that we had all that out yesterday?'

Her heart was thudding, but she managed a glittering smile. 'I know, I know, but I decided to come just the same. It's no use telling me not to, because I'll follow you—all the way!' Her blue eyes sparkled with anger and she was unaware that she looked very young and vulnerable.

'The devil you will!' A reluctant smile hovered at the corners of his mouth. 'Okay then, you can tag along if you like—if you can last the distance!'

'I will.'

They went through a gate, up a rise, then rode into the splendour of the sunrise. The atmosphere was incredibly clear and a chorus of birdsong filled the air. As they went on Jacqui was content just to be here. Could it be the matter of having gained her objective that gave her this feeling of heightened awareness, as if the surroundings were bathed in a golden light? For a time they took the Land Rover track over the hills, then as the sun blazed into the heat of summer they turned down towards a bush-filled gully. Soon they were riding in the filtered sunlight, the horses' hooves silent on the damp moss and leaves

underfoot. Brad rode ahead, pulling back from the twisting path long trails of creepers and trailing black
supplejack that barred their way. It was a fragrant world,
heavy with the damp pungent smell of the bush, crowded
with fivefinger and fern and the drooping fronds of lacy
pungas. Jacqui recognised the flute-like double note of the
tui and caught a glimpse of the bird with its iridescent
feathers and white throat, high above.

They emerged at last into brilliant sunshine, urging
their horses to a canter on the green slopes, while sheep
scattered in panic. All at once a rabbit scampered under
Prince's hoof and the horse shied violently. This time,
however, Jacqui too had caught sight of the small creature
and as the horse swung to the side, she kept her seat.
After a moment she realised that Brad had pulled his
mount to a trot and was looking at her in surprise. Had
he really expected her to bail out—again? He made no
comment, however, so she said nothing.

She realised now how hopeless it would have been for
her to have attempted the journey alone. They swept over
flat stretches, to dip down into gullies. Then they were
following a leaf-choked stream, to once again take sheep-
dotted slopes in a route that seemed to her to lead ever
farther from civilisation.

As the time went by she became aware of Brad's swift
enquiring glances in her direction. Did he expect her to
beg for a rest, or to return to the homestead? They had
pulled their mounts to a walk and were riding abreast
when at last she taxed him. 'I'm still here. How far do we
have to go now?'

'We're about half way.' For a moment his gaze
softened. 'Think you can make it?'

'Half way already? My goodness,' deliberately she made
her tone disbelieving, 'I thought the trip would be much
farther! I'm a country girl at heart, remember?'

'So you told me.' At the derision in his tone she had to
school herself not to let the anger show. Instead she said
lightly, 'Whatever gave you the idea that I'd flake out at

any moment?' *I bet your Sue would think nothing of it!*

He seemed to pick up her thoughts. 'Lots of girls would. Not Sue, of course, she'd take it in her stride.'

Sue would, Jacqui thought vindictively. Aloud she demanded: 'What makes you think I won't last the distance? Is it because I'm small? Something about the way I look?'

She saw a light leap into his eyes. 'Oh no, Jacqui, there's nothing wrong with the way you look.' His appreciative gaze swept her face, flushed from exertion and the heat of the day. Jacqui had the incredible feeling that not only was he gazing at her but sending out signals that gave her a sense of triumph. Just for once he had betrayed himself. His gaze travelled down to the apricot-tan of her throat between the deep V of her blouse.

Because she just knew he would qualify the statement the next moment, she cut in lightly, 'Oh well, I guess that's something!'

Crazy, the way the sunshine seemed so much brighter than on any other day she'd been at the station. Could it be this heightened sense of awareness she felt today? And Brad imagined she would be exhausted by the cross-country ride. The way she was feeling right at this moment she could ride on for ever.

Over the next rise they reined in, gazing down towards a small lake where the overhanging trees met their own reflections in the limpid depths. Then they were riding down the slope and following the contour of the lake.

'The old-time Maoris knew something when they christened this lake Waiwhetu.' Jacqui spoke idly, her eyes on the placid water.

He nodded. 'Star Water. On a clear night you can see the reflections from the sky.'

'I'd love to see it like that!' The next moment she would have given anything to recall the impulsive words. Would he think she was working towards a midnight rendezvous with him?

And of course that was just what he did think. 'Stick

around,' he advised coolly, 'and you might get Chris to bring you over some fine night!'

'Chris?' She turned towards him blue eyes sparkling with indignation. As she had expected, his face wore a far from teasing expression and it was only with an effort of will she bit back the angry rejoinder that trembled on her lips. 'You never let up on him, do you?'

Brad made no answer.

One more week, she consoled herself, just seven more days and he'll know the truth. Maybe then he'll realise that the boss can make mistakes, and whoppers at that!

Could it be the cloud passing over the sun that made her imagine the golden day had lost a little of its lustre? All at once she was feeling hot and weary and her limbs were stiff and aching. Not that she would admit such a weakness to him. It seemed a long way to their destination, but when at last they came in sight of the cottage, her spirits revived. Now perhaps she could vindicate Nick, and herself. There'd be a letter awaiting her at Te Kainga, of course there would!

When they reached the cottage, she pulled rein. 'I can't wait to take a look in that letter box up the road.'

'It's up to you.' He seemed scarcely interested in the matter. 'If everything's okay up on the bush farm I'll be back in an hour. If not I'll be some time.'

Jacqui scarcely heard his words. Suddenly all the tiredness had left her limbs and she set her mount to a canter along the rough metal road.

The wooden box nailed to a post proved a disappointment, for even as she riffled through an assortment of outdated newspapers and folders, she knew there was no letter among the papers, not even an account for Nick. But there was still hope. As she slipped down from the saddle—who would have thought she would feel so stiff after a ride?—she tethered Prince on the grass and followed a trail of newspapers, yellowed by exposure to the weather, that the wind had blown beneath trees and into low bushes. Wildly she searched among the greenery,

as far away as a barbed wire fence with its tatters of
sheep's wool blowing in the breeze. She was on the point
of turning away when a glimpse of white caught her eye
and she pulled from a blackberry bush an envelope,
sodden with rain, but she could make out her own name.
Carefully she slit open the envelope. If only the letter
wasn't too wet and damaged to be legible! But it was all
right, she thought in relief as Nick's bold black script
swam before her eyes. A few words had run together, but
the main part was intact and all too clear.

   'Hi, Brat,

          I'm posting this from Auckland airport. Just
had a thought you might turn up at the cottage and find
the bird has flown. This should get to you in time. Not
my fault I'm off in a hurry. You can blame the big boss
up on the hill. He kicked me out, no second chance, no
mercy, just—get going or else! So here I am on the way
to Canada to try my luck over there! Too bad you missed
out on your farm holiday, but you're due for a break in
Kiwi-land, so—enjoy, enjoy!

   I'll drop you a line when I get myself an address in
Canada. Put you in the picture about what's happened at
Te Kainga. Meantime, take my advice and get out of the
place *fast*, before Brad starts in on you too. I don't think
he cares much for our family. See you some time, Nick.'

   The sense of let-down hit her like a blow, and the words
swam before her eyes in a mist of tears. Just that! No
word of the money he owed Brad because of the lease, no
mention of the repayment of her own investment in the
venture. She crushed the damp sheet of paper to a ball in
her hand, for she knew the words were already branded
on her brain with cruel emphasis.

   A tiny flicker of doubt rose in her mind, but she pushed
it aside. Nick had written in a hurry. He'd scribbled her a
note at the airport and he'd explain later, he'd said he
would. All he had wanted was to warn her about the
most important matter, about Brad.

Slowly, slowly, she retraced her steps, then pulled herself up to the saddle. The road to the cottage seemed to go on forever and she had an odd sensation of floating . . . fatigue, hunger, the awful sense of let-down? When she reached the small dwelling she let herself in and told herself that she had one thing for which she was thankful, and that was that Brad was nowhere in sight.

Outside she watered her horse and left him to graze. Inside the cottage was hot and airless. Jacqui dropped to a chair by the table and dropped her head on her crossed arms. She had been so certain that Nick's letter would put everything right. Instead—without warning the tears came, spilling down her flushed cheeks and trickling through her fingers. The sobs were still shaking her when Brad's quiet tones penetrated the fog of misery.

'It's a tough ride in the heat, takes it out of you.'

She raised drowned blue eyes to his face. To think she had let him find her in this state! Wildly she brushed her hand across her eyes, leaving a long smudge of dust on her cheeks. 'It's not that,' she muttered.

'What, then?'

'I haven't got a hankie.'

He proffered a spotless white square from his shirt pocket. 'Come on, blow!'

Weakly she complied. Then she pushed the hair back from her damp forehead.

Brad dropped to straddle a chair and she was uncomfortably aware of his narrowed glance. 'You look as though you've been having a rough time,' his voice was very gentle. 'What's the problem?'

She moistened dry lips. 'N—nothing.'

'Come on, you can't get away with that, not with me!'

He was determined to probe, damn him, merely no doubt for the satisfaction of rubbing it in.

'You didn't come across any letter because there wasn't one, is that it?'

She had an impulse to lie, but what was the use? He would dig the truth out of her, he had that look about him.

She raised a tear-stained face. 'I found a letter,' she admitted, 'it was ever so old, written before I got here. It was all wet and dirty, but I managed to read it.'

'Did you now?' She caught the narrowing of his eyes. 'Was it worth making the trip for, do you think?'

His mocking tone sparked her to reply hotly, 'Of course it was! That's what I came for, wasn't it?' Immediately she spoilt the brave words by adding with a rush, 'Only it didn't tell me anything I don't know already. It was so out of date ... and my not getting it until weeks later, like this. But he promised to write me as soon as he got an address in Canada where I could contact him.'

'Is that so?' His tone was sceptical. 'Taking his time, isn't he?'

'You don't understand!' To her chagrin she felt the stupid tears misting her eyes. She got to her feet, anxious to escape his too-observant glance. Tears would be just what he'd enjoy. Hadn't he advised her not to come here, but she had insisted on making the journey. Now he had the edge on her and no doubt intended to take full advantage of it. Wildly she made to hurry out of the room. 'I've got to see to Prince——'

'He's okay!' He was blocking her escape. 'For Pete's sake,' he caught her hands in his tight grip, 'quit running away and listen to me! Why not open your eyes, face up to the truth for a change?'

'I know what you're going to say!' she cried. 'Don't bother!' She struggled wildly in his grasp, but he held her in an iron grip. 'Let me go! Take your hands off me!'

'Do you really want me to?'

How did it happen? She was caught close to him and a tumultuous excitement was pounding through her pulses.

His low tones, hoarse with emotion, reached her. 'Jacqui, look at me!'

Impelled by something beyond her control, she raised her gaze—to his tanned chest revealed by his shirt, unbuttoned to the waist, the tousled dark hair. He looked dusty and hot, and infinitely desirable. A melting sweetness ran through her and as his lips found hers every other thought melted away in the wild fire that ran along her nerves.

At last he released her and in the heady excitement of the moment it took a moment or so for her to come back to reality. She looked up to meet his gaze, softened now, but she caught a flicker of triumph in his eyes. All the happiness of the moment fled and she turned away abruptly. 'If you think,' she whispered, 'that you can change my mind about Nick and you and everything, *that* way——'

He grinned, he was actually grinning as though he had gained a victory after all. 'No harm in trying!'

Oh, she might have known he was just amusing himself, taking advantage of a sunshiny day and a girl he didn't find too unattractive to kiss! If only he didn't have this disturbing, heart-stopping effect on her. The thoughts rushed through her mind, he had only to touch her and her defences melted away. She became aware that he was eyeing her with something like amusement—*amusement!* She said, 'I'll go and see if Prince is all right,' and this time he made no attempt to detain her.

A quick glance assured her that her mount was quite all right, she had known he would be really. At the tank-stand she washed away the heat and dust of the long ride and splashed rainwater on her reddened eyes. When she came back into the room Brad appeared just as usual, as though no emotion had flared briefly between them. He was pouring steaming liquid from a flask into two coffee mugs. 'Lunch is on!' He opened a packet of sandwiches and placed them on the table. 'I don't know what they are, but Mrs Beeson usually makes things taste pretty good. Try one.'

'I seem to be always eating your lunch!' but Jacqui dropped down to a stool and sipped the hot coffee.

'Not to worry, she's used to hefty appetites and you never know who's going to turn up to join you on a day's ride.'

Like herself? To Brad she was a mere passing incident. What had she expected of him, for heaven's sake? She knew that a kiss was just a kiss, didn't she?

'Take it easy,' he told her a little later. 'I'm off up the hill to see how things are up there, but if everything's okay I won't be long.' His tone softened. 'You'll be all right?'

'Of course I will!' she said with spirit.

From the window she watched him ride up the green slope. To think she had weakly allowed him to find her in this sorry state. Now he would think she wasn't capable of the long ride that Sue 'would have taken in her stride!' Her thoughts spun round in aimless circles. She would have been perfectly all right if it hadn't been for finding Nick's letter. It was the shock and let-down of the contents that had made her give way to that storm of weeping. And before him! She could have kicked herself!

He was back before half an hour had passed and soon they were riding away from the cottage. As the miles of the homeward ride fell away they spoke little, but it seemed to Jacqui that they rode with a sense of companionship, or was that her imagination? Something to do with the clear bright sunshine, the feeling of remoteness and the pleasure of the moment. For oddly all her tiredness had left her and aches and stiffness were forgotten in the exhilaration of galloping over green stretches, her hair flying behind her ears.

They had pulled their mounts to a walk and were riding together when he said: 'I have to hand it to you, you're a top rider, long distance and all!'

A wave of happiness surged through her, but she tried to make her tone offhanded. 'I've done it before, lots of times, on the farm at home. And I did have a good horse!' She leaned forward to pat Prince's sweat-stained neck. 'We understand each other, even if we did get off to a bad start.'

'Which is more than you could say for us!'

She sent him a quick surprised glance, but he was smil-

ing. For the very first time in their stormy acquaintance
he was looking towards her as if she were just any girl he
happened to know, and not Nick's scheming young sister.

The excited feeling lasted until they were in sight of the
homestead, and Jacqui caught sight of a horseman can-
tering over the paddocks. At first she took the rider for
one of the stockmen, but very soon she recognised the
feminine figure. Sue coming to meet Brad.

They met at the foot of the slope beside a thicket of
cabbage trees. That was, Jacqui thought, the other two
riders met. For beyond a cursory glance, Sue totally
ignored Jacqui. The other girl's flawless make-up and
shining blonde hair made Jacqui all too aware of her
dishevelled appearance. Not that Brad would notice what
she looked like. His attention was all for the girl holding
in the mettlesome chestnut. What was Sue going on
about? Something to do with a world-famous show-jumper
who was arriving from England by air and would stay at
her parents' home? Sue had met him in England last year,
when they were both competing in show-jumping cham-
pionships. He was in the country with the object of buying
horses and she would like Brad to be at the house tomorrow to meet him. Jacqui was barely aware of Sue's deep
forceful tones.

As they rode back towards the homestead Jacqui
thought irritatedly that she might just as well not have
been there, the other two were so complete in their own
private world.

CHAPTER TEN

THAT night Jacqui changed for dinner into a crisp white cotton frock that was splashed with scarlet tropical flowers. She needed something gay and bright, she told herself, after the crazy ups and downs of the frustrating day. So few days left for her here at Waiwhetu now . . . she paused, a perfume spray in her hand, her thoughts drifting. It must be because of Nick having lived here that she felt attached to the place. The place, or the owner? The truth hit her like a blow. She couldn't love him, not Brad. She loathed him—or tried to. You couldn't love a man you couldn't trust. It was his aura of power and arrogant good looks that had blinded her to his real character. She must keep telling herself that or she was lost.

At the dinner table Bernice was with a lanky, serious-eyed young man wearing a city suit. 'This is Luke,' she said to Jacqui. 'I didn't know he was coming.' The teacher, Jacqui thought, the persistent suitor who was waiting for Bernice to make up her mind. Throughout the meal he said little, picking at the succulent roast lamb and green peas on his plate, and feasting his eyes on Bernice as if he could never see enough of her.

Tonight there was no danger of her meeting Brad's sardonic glance. He and Sue were seated side by side, her deep tones echoing around the table as she held forth on the merits of the visiting show-jumping champion to her home.

'I do hope you can stay longer than one night, Luke,' Bernice's mother said to Luke. 'I'm sure Bernice has missed you—' At a warning frown from her daughter she broke off. After a moment she rallied, saying with a smile, 'Can't you stay a bit longer while you're here?'

'I—' Luke was looking embarrassed. 'It all depends,' he said in a low tone, 'on Bernice.'

Jacqui realised that Rick, easy-going, happy-go-lucky Rick, was suddenly alert, his gaze flicking from Bernice to Luke, and she knew that he was listening intently.

'Thing is,' Luke explained, 'I've got an appointment overseas in the teaching line, something I always hoped to get, but I never dreamed it would come my way.'

'Congratulations!' There was a chorus from around the table. Aunt Tessa said with a smile, 'You'll be a great success, I know!'

He smiled deprecatingly. 'Hope so! I'll do my best. The only snag is,' he went on slowly, 'I've got to start in Canada earlier than I thought, next week actually. I've just come to say goodbye, unless . . .' His voice trailed away and Bernice said with a nervous giggle,

'There's a friend for you! All that way!'

Jacqui hoped that Rick would put his own interpretation on Luke's words.

When the meal was over, Bernice and Luke wandered down the steps and sauntered up a slope, in the gathering dusk. A long time later when Jacqui was reading in bed— or trying to, for Brad's mocking smile kept coming between her mind and the printed words and she kept remembering the sensuous delight of being caught close in his arms—she heard a tap on the door.

'Can I come in?' Bernice's voice was followed by a dark head pushed around the door. Flushed and excited, she dropped down to the bed. 'I had to talk to someone, I feel so awful. Luke looked all cut up, but I had to do it.' The words came in broken sentences. 'It wouldn't have been fair to him. The funny thing is that he guessed about Rick. He told me he'd always known there was someone and as soon as he saw us together he knew who it was, that he hadn't any chance. If only he hadn't been so nice about it, wishing me luck, and for all I know the loving is all one-sided. But I can't help it. There's just no one else for me, and whether he loves me or not makes no difference!'

'I know,' Jacqui spoke her thoughts aloud, 'love's the

devil, isn't it?' Bernice looked surprised and Jacqui quickly changed the subject. 'Who knows, you may never leave here. Happy ever after? I wouldn't be surprised!'

Bernice's face took on a radiance. 'You'll be the first one asked to the wedding.' Her eyes shadowed. 'If there is a wedding——'

'Bernice, you in there?' Rick's voice cut across her words.

'Just coming.' A wave of her hand and she closed the door behind her. Jacqui couldn't help but overhear Rick's urgent tones. 'Luke's just taken off hell for leather in his car, zoomed down the road as if he was possessed by the devil! When I couldn't find you I got worried—Look, honey, I've got to thinking there are things we've got to talk over. You see, darling——' The voices drifted away as the other two moved down the passage, and Jacqui's soft lips quirked.

She wasn't surprised when the next day Rick and Bernice announced their engagement to the family. A cloud of happiness suffused them and everyone wished them well. 'This calls for champagne,' said Brad, and handed around the drinks. Toasts were drunk and the young couple were plied with eager questions. When was the wedding? Where would it be held? Rick held up a restraining hand. 'Taiho—we haven't got around to arrangements yet. I'll tell you this much, though.' He drew Bernice into the shelter of his arm. 'We've only just found out that we've loved each other for ages. We're off to town tomorrow to choose the ring—that is,' he threw a half laughing, half serious glance towards Brad, 'unless you'd like to pass on the family one, the diamonds and ruby job that you've been hanging on to all these years.'

'Sorry,' Brad's even tones gave nothing away, 'but I'll be needing it myself any time now.'

The words fell into a startled silence. Rick stared at his brother in amazement. 'You've been holding out on us!'

Jacqui felt a pain that was almost physical pierce her. Everyone knew about Brad and Sue, took it for granted

that they would eventually marry, so why did the fact of
putting it into words hurt so much?

She raised heavy eyes to meet Brad's brooding glance
and for a sickening moment she wondered if her expression
had given her away.

Even Chris, these days so wrapped up in his own plans,
looked surprised. 'You might let us in on it,' he com-
plained.

'I will when the time's right.' There was a finality in
Brad's tone that discouraged further questioning.

The sooner I get away from here the better, Jacqui
told herself, but deep down she knew that she would cling
to the few remaining days until the last minute, fool that
she was. If this was what love did to you ... her gaze
moved to Rick and Bernice. Love could be wonderful,
the most wonderful thing in the world, but it wasn't for
her.

On the day of the art exhibition in town, no one at the
homestead seemed particularly interested in Chris and
Jacqui's departure. Earlier in the day, Jacqui had caught
sight of Brad driving his Land Rover in the direction of
the main road, no doubt on the way to Sue's home to
meet the English show-jumping champion. Or was that
merely an excuse on Sue's part? she wondered. The route
was becoming familiar to her and they were nearing the
thermal city when an ominous clanking sound met their
ears and she heard Chris's muttered oath. 'I'll have to
put in at the nearest garage. I'll drop you at the gallery
and I'll meet you inside.' He gave a forced laugh. 'Think
I'll be able to find you in the mob?'

'Don't be such a pessimist!' When they reached The
Gallery he kept the engine running and Jacqui got out of
the car, then went in at the open doors where people
were milling around the pictures hanging on the walls.
Her first impression was that the artwork was well displayed in the light streaming in at the windows. There
seemed a crowd in the room and as she wandered past

the paintings she caught snatches of comments. 'An un-usual technique . . . quite unique treatment of water and light . . . He has a future ahead of him. Who is he?' All at once she realised she was facing her own portrait. The red sticker told her it had already been sold. Had she really looked like that? she wondered wistfully. There was an elusive happiness in her half-smile, her eyes glimmered with a secret happiness, like a girl in love. Why hadn't she picked up the signals then and taken herself far away from Brad and his arrogant masculine attraction? From his kisses that had awakened her to feelings she had never before experienced, leaving with her a hunger there was no assuaging.

She moved on, weaving her way between the groups strolling along the carpeted floor. Then all at once a canvas arrested her. Of course, Nick's cottage at Te Kainga—correction, Brad's cottage. She recognised the little wooden building with its backdrop of hills, bush-clad, range after range, fading into the blue distance. There was the water tank, the tangle of bushes encroach-ing on the back door that Nick had never had time to clear.

'It's Te Kainga! A run-off miles and miles away, up in the hills!' She spun around to face a slim girl with a bub-bling excited voice and a cloud of blonde hair, a girl whose face seemed vaguely familiar, yet she couldn't ever have met her. Aloud she asked with a smile, 'You know it?'

A wry smile twisted the wide red lips. 'Do I ever!' She eyed Jacqui with her friendly smile. 'You're a stranger in Rotorua?'

'Yes, but——'

'Look, you're not serious about this picture, are you? I mean, you're not thinking of buying it?'

Jacqui knew she had no need to buy the painting, for the lonely cottage would be imprinted clearly on her mind. It would be far more difficult to make herself forget. 'No, not at these prices!'

'I know how you feel, but the paintings are worth it! And someone's already bought the highest priced one of the showing, someone's portrait. The buyer must have money to burn! Come to think of it,' she looked at Jacqui thoughtfully, 'the picture looks a lot like you. It looks as if by the end of the week the whole lot will have found buyers!' She added in a low tone, 'It's time he had some luck. He could do with it!'

Jacqui said, surprised, 'You know the artist?'

'I used to—once—Look, I've got to talk to someone or go out of my skull. If you could put up with me, how about coffee? There's a little place down the road. I should know, I used to work there.'

'Love to.'

The other girl chatted as they moved out of the door and into the sun-drenched street. 'I didn't think I'd ever be coming back here. I scarcely know a soul, even the coffee bar has changed hands since I've been away, and the staff are different too. Funny how you expect things to be just the same, you hope—' Her voice broke. 'Here we are!' The decor of the place was attractive, Jacqui thought, looking around at the stained woodwork and shaded lamps. The fair-haired girl chose a corner table and ordered coffee. As they sipped the steaming liquid it seemed to Jacqui that the other girl's face shed the laughing mask, leaving her looking pinched and anxious. 'You must think I'm crazy,' she sent Jacqui a tremulous smile, 'dragging you in here. Why should you want to hear all my troubles anyway? Guess you've got enough of your own!'

You've guessed right. Jacqui made the observation silently. Aloud she said gently, 'You can tell me. I scarcely know anyone around Rotorua and I'll be leaving for good in a few days anyway.'

The blonde head was bent over the coffee mug. 'If only I hadn't met up with Nick—Oh, don't get me wrong,' she said quickly, 'he was so *nice*! You know what I mean? When you were with him he made you feel you were the only girl in the whole world. Just being with him . . . I don't know . . . there's something about him, even the way he was.'

Nick! It couldn't be *her* Nick! The thoughts whirled through Jacqui's mind.

She wrenched her mind back to the light tones. 'Funny, isn't it, even when you find someone out for what they are, untrustworthy and all that, you still can't get him out of your mind.'

Jacqui sat very still. At that moment there flashed across the screen of her mind a photograph of a laughing blonde girl and Nick. Nick and Lorraine. Now that she knew the girl's identity was it fair to let her go on?

It was too late. Lorraine's voice, throbbing with emotion, was running on. 'I fell in love with Nick, in one week, I really loved him. Could you believe that? Infatuation, isn't that what they call it? It just sweeps you away, and afterwards, you come down to earth.' She plucked nervously at her dress. 'I had the real thing once, and I threw it away. I'd have done anything for Nick, somehow he made life such *fun*! When you were with him you believed every word he said.' Her eyes were abstracted. 'Even that story he told me about the man he leased the cottage from kicking him out without giving him a chance to pay the money for the lease he owed him. I was so besotted with Nick I told him about my aunt and uncle over in Canada. They had a big ranch there and they'd often asked me over for a holiday, though I'd never taken up their offer. I knew they wouldn't mind my taking another guest for a few weeks and I told Nick that maybe they could put him in the way of some work on their property.' A bitter smile curved her lips. 'If only I'd known!'

Jacqui was very pale. 'What happened? Weren't you welcome when you arrived there?'

'Oh, we were welcome all right. My relatives were wonderful, they couldn't do enough for us. The trouble was that Nick's fatal charm was turned on full beam—

why not, he had a lot at stake. My cousin Mary, an only child, plain and ordinary-looking and not very young, but what did that matter to Nick when some day she would inherit the ranch and everything else. He really went to work on Mary. In a way I couldn't blame her for falling for him in a big way. My uncle and aunt weren't much in favour of her feelings for him, they were worried about how I felt about Nick's sudden change of heart.

'So then I knew it was time for me to get out and leave the field clear. I had this battle with myself whether or not to put my relatives wise about Nick—I was beginning to see through his lies and evasions by that time, then I thought maybe I'd keep quiet about what I knew. It wasn't as if he'd hurt anyone, except me, and he wasn't really bad, only determined to make money without working for it. I sort of felt that if he had a rich wife and the life he wanted he'd be satisfied. With Mary and no money worries he'd relax and there'd be no more scheming and lying and acting, and everyone would be happy, except me, of course.'

After a pause she went on, 'So I came back here, heaven knows why. Except that deep down I had this feeling about Chris. I wanted to tell him I'm sorry about . . . what happened. Poor Chris, the day I got back here I ran into someone I used to know and she told me he'd had a nervous breakdown after I—well, threw him over for Nick, just when he was all starry-eyed over wedding arrangements. He's a quiet, intense sort of guy, takes things very seriously.' She went on slowly, thoughtfully, 'I guess I've begun to realise too late that any girl who has someone like Chris, who really *cares*, is pretty lucky. And I tossed it aside! I've been trying for days to nerve myself to ring him up and tell him. Once I even got as far as a phone booth, but I got a wrong number and I didn't have the courage to try again. Then I heard that he was opening this exhibition of his paintings. I couldn't believe it! But it meant he wasn't ill any more. I had a crazy notion that if I hung around there he might come in and—I don't know. He might not even want to see me, what do you think?'

'Give it a go!' urged Jacqui. 'He'll be coming in to The Gallery today——'

Lorraine looked up in surprise. 'How do you know?'

'Oh, he's sure to be, on the opening day. Any artist would make certain of that! And don't worry about him not wanting you——'

Again the other girl looked puzzled. 'What makes you think he'll feel that way?'

'I just—know.'

'Do you really think so?' A light of hope sprang into Lorraine's eyes. 'I'm fond of him, not like it was with Nick, all wildfire and excitement ... It's different. But I'm happy and contented when I'm with Chris. If only,' she sighed wistfully, 'we could start all over again where we left off.' Her expression brightened. 'I'm going back to The Gallery. If you think I've got a chance at happiness, she was gathering up her bag, 'what am I doing here? Finished your coffee? Do you mind if I run away back to The Gallery? Who knows,' a tremulous smile touched her lips, 'this might just turn out to be my day!'

'Wait just a moment.' At the urgency in Jacqui's tone, Lorraine paused. 'Just one thing before you go. That Nick—what did you mean about his being "the way he was"?'

'Oh, that?' Lorraine dropped back on her seat, her eyes thoughtful. 'I thought you'd get what I meant. He was so darn cruel, quite ruthless about anything that interfered with his plans. It was just as if he were two people. When he was getting everything he wanted, and that meant money, he was charming. But the other side of Nick ... He had a young sister in England he used to tell me about. He thought it was hilarious that he'd managed so easily to get her share of the money their father had left them. She's soft as butter, he used to say, a silly little dope who believes everything I tell her, always has. The trick is to condition anyone like that. I trained her young, you see.

It was easy. Now it's a habit with her to think every word I tell her is gospel. He used to say that if he played his cards right he might work the hat trick again, but he'd have to wait until she'd saved up a bit.

'When the sister wrote and said she was coming out here to join him he was really in a spot. He was scared stiff that the sheep farmer who owns the run-off, a man called Brad Kent, would let his sister in to the truth about Nick. But he took care of that by writing his sister— Jacqui, he called her—all sorts of lies about the man who owns Te Kainga. He said his sister would never believe anyone else's story if he'd got in first. He told me it was the easiest thing in the world to manipulate her. "I've only got to ask her," he used to say, "and she falls over herself to help me." I guess,' she added on a sigh, 'I was just about the same way myself. It was the way he used to laugh about his sister that got me. Then one day I got to thinking, would he treat me like that too? Throw me over if he met a girl with money? And he did—and the funny thing was,' her voice broke, 'that I was the one who made it happen!'

Jacqui said very low, 'You might be lucky at that!'

Lorraine squared her shoulders. There seemed to be a new light of purpose in her eyes. 'You think it's worth while my waiting around at The Gallery today?'

'Oh, definitely!' It was an effort for Jacqui to gather her thoughts together. 'Don't bother about me, I'll have another cup.'

For a moment the fair girl hesitated, as she took in the pallor of Jacqui's face. 'You're feeling all right, aren't you? You look sort of . . . funny. Because if you're not——'

'No, no, it's nothing. Just a headache, I get them sometimes. It's the heat, I guess. Nothing to worry about.'

'If you say so. Goodbye, then!'

'Good luck,' Jacqui whispered.

She never knew how long she sat on at the table, unaware of customers at nearby tables who threw curious glances towards the girl with the odd dazed expression, seated alone. Cold shivers of shock were running through her and she was unaware of the concern of a kindly waitress. 'Would you care for another cup of coffee?'

'Coffee?' Jacqui's blue eyes held a curious blankness. 'No, no, thank you.'

Some time later the thought penetrated her dazed senses that the room was becoming crowded with shoppers and sightseers, and she got up and wandered out into the clear bright sunshine of the street, uncaring of where her random steps were taking her. Brad, Brad, she thought, you tried to tell me the truth and I accused *you* of lying! I was so sure of myself, so blind to Nick's real nature that I refused to listen to you, and now it's too late!

Oblivious of the holiday crowd surging around her, she moved blindly along the main street of the city. It must be because she loved him so that she imagined his vibrant tones calling her name.

'Jacqui!' She realised that a dust-smeared Land Rover had drawn up at her side and Brad leaned from the driver's seat. 'Hop in!' He flung open the passenger door and she climbed in beside him.

'It *is* you!' She turned an expressionless face towards him. Freshly groomed, smiling, at ease with himself and the world, she thought he had never seemed to her more attractive—or unattainable. 'I thought,' she said dazedly, 'that you were with Súe today. What are you doing in Rotorua?' She'd betrayed herself, of course, but nothing mattered any more. How could she have believed him capable of cruelty and deceit? She only had to look at his face as he was at this moment . . .

He made no move to start the vehicle.

'Looking for you.' Even in her miasma of misery, his sense of excited happiness came through. What could have happened to put him in this exalted mood? She realised that he was eyeing her closely. 'You're feeling all right, Jacqui?' His tone was strangely gentle. 'I've never seen you so pale.'

'It's the heat,' she said quickly. 'I thought I'd get out

in the open air and just walk around for a while. A head-ache . . .'

'Was that it? I ran into Chris at The Gallery and he told me you'd arranged to meet him there but there'd been some slip-up. So I offered to go and see where you'd got to.' Brad grinned. 'That was a couple of hours ago.'

'Oh, my goodness!' her hand flew guiltily to her mouth. 'I should have left a message for Chris. Was he worried—about me?'

He grinned. 'Not so you'd notice. He was pretty well taken up with his own affairs when I left him.'

Jacqui roused herself from her heavy thoughts. 'You knew about the exhibition of Chris's paintings, then?'

He nodded. 'Had a ring late last night from a mate of mine, putting me in the picture.' Once again she was aware of an air of excitement about him. 'You didn't really think you could keep a secret from me, young Jacqui? Don't tell me it was all Chris's idea, the big sur-prise?'

'Only until he had some sales! You were too hard on him,' she burst out, 'you didn't give him a word of en-couragement, none of you did. It made him feel inept and hopeless, especially after——'

'You've no need to waste any sympathy on him,' Brad's tone was brusque. 'He's doing fine, judging by the crowd in The Gallery a while ago. Want to go back there and have a look around? I gather that the pictures are pretty familiar to you. Chris tells me you organised the whole thing, practically shoved him into holding the exhibition.'

'I didn't do anything much, I just—believed in him.'

'Is that all?' His voice was cryptic. 'Want to take an-other look around?'

She shook her head. 'I did go through The Gallery before Chris got there. It was quite early then—and do you know,' she roused herself to concentrate on the pres-ent, 'one picture was sold already, the highest priced one of the lot too! A mystery buyer, they said.'

'I know,' Brad's face was deadpan. 'I made certain no

one else was going to beat me to that portrait of you!'

'Me?' Jerked from her abstraction she glanced up in surprise. 'Why would you—?' She stopped short, a flood of colour staining her cheeks. 'But of course,' she hurried on, 'you would want to give Chris some encouragement . . . his first showing. He's really going places, you know. All he needed was a chance—and a bit of luck.'

'He's got that too.' Brad's well shaped lips tilted at the corners. 'If you could see him at this moment! I doubt if he's more happy about the exhibition or his meeting up again with Lorraine. There'll be no holding him from now on!' Could that be the reason for his elation? she wondered. Lorraine's infatuation for Nick had ended and she had come back to Chris. Another victory for Brad! Unconsciously she sighed.

She realised he had put a hand to the starter motor. 'Let's go home, shall we?'

She nodded, no longer caring where she was, longing only to be with him.

Watching his lean bronzed hand on the steering wheel, she knew that never again in all her life might she feel like this about a man. Soon it would be time for her to go. The thought made her say, 'Pancho's nearly better now. I don't need to stay . . . any longer.'

'Let's talk it over, shall we?' There was an odd note of urgency in his tone and he put his foot down harder on the accelerator. They had left the city behind and were climbing a road cutting between cleared green hills. 'There are one or two things we've got to get straight between us, young Jacqui!' He flicked her a sideways glance, his eyes deep and soft, almost as if he had kissed her. She scarcely recognised him in this odd exuberant state of mind.

'Anyone would think,' she sent him a tremulous smile, 'that it was your big day, instead of Chris's.'

'But it is! Didn't I tell you?' Brad threw an arm around her shoulders, and as always his touch started the trembling in her. Today she made no move to avoid him.

Such little things, his touch, his kisses, to last her for the rest of her life.

She said on a breath, 'Sue——?' Once again she had betrayed herself. Stupid! Stupid! Shock and despair must have slowed down her reactions.

He merely laughed, a chuckle deep in his throat. 'Guess again!'

Should she tell him, she wondered, all that she had learned today from Lorraine? Not at this moment, she decided, for tears threatened and if she should break down now ... What did it matter to him anyway? She blinked away the moisture from her eyes. To him she was no more than a casual visitor he had put up at the homestead for a short time.

As the miles fell away there was silence between them. A long time later she came out of bitter musing to realise they were taking an unfamiliar turning. 'But this isn't the way home!'

'It is you know. *My way!*' They sped down a dusty track to come in sight of the shimmering jewel-like lake far below. 'My favourite lake!'

'Mine too, but—why today?'

'Shall I tell you the answer to that one?' Brad's arm tightened around her shoulders and his tones were alive with a sense of urgency. 'Because I wanted to get you to myself.'

Jacqui's heart gave a great leap and all at once the frustrations and fears of the day vanished. They hurtled down the pathway and he braked in a clearing. The next moment he was getting down from the vehicle, flinging open the passenger door. His eyes, looking into hers, were brilliant. 'Come on!' He took her hand in his strong grasp and drew her along a narrow twisting track through the bush. Brad, so impetuous, in such haste, so exuberent ... what could have happened today to have put him in this most un-Bradlike mood? At last they pushed their way through ferns to reach the water's edge and, breathless and laughing, threw themselves down on the green grass.

It was very still, the only sound the soft splash of wavelets on the shore.

'*Now*, my darling,' he said softly, and turned to take her in his arms. His lips brushed the contours of her face, her throat, to claim her mouth in a kiss that sent her pulses rocketing. 'If you only knew,' his voice was husky with emotion, 'how I've longed for this!'

A long time later, shaken, her eyes soft and dreamy, Jacqui gazed up in his arms, raising a hand to trace the strong line of his jaw. 'A goodbye kiss?' She had meant the words to sound light and carefree, but they emerged in a broken whisper.

'Never!' His gaze lingered on her as if he were drinking in every line of her troubled young face. 'It's just for starters, to alter your mind about your brother and all that stuff—Look at me,' his hard muscular body was pressed close to hers. 'Do you still think I'd be so rough on a tenant of mine?'

'Why,' she whispered, 'do you want me to answer that?'

'For the same reason, my darling, that I went in hell-for-leather today to make sure of getting that portrait of you! I was so damned scared of losing you. Knowing the truth about Chris and his pictures gave me the go-ahead, now all I have to do is make you understand. It's up to you now,' his voice held a strong demanding note, 'whose word are you going to take, your brother Nick's—or mine?'

A thousand golden splinters of sunshine were making Jacqui blink her eyes, or could it be the radiance splintering all around her? 'You!' she said promptly, and burst into laughter at the amazement in his face.

'Just one kiss persuaded you?' he asked softly.

'And the others,' she amended. 'You don't think I could ever forget Emerald Cave?'

'I love you.' He bent his dark head to claim her lips. When she could speak she said in a muffled tone, 'Of course, running into Lorraine in The Gallery this morning opened my eyes, made all the difference.'

His eyes glimmered softly and he carried her hand to his lips. 'So that was it?'

She nodded. 'I got such a shock, but I guess,' she added thoughtfully, 'I was due for a rude awakening. Worshipping anyone like I did Nick was asking for trouble. I couldn't, wouldn't believe that what you told me was for real. I suppose,' she admitted laughingly, 'I was pretty stubborn!'

'You've got all the rest of your life to make it up to me,' he told her teasingly. 'No more talk of going away, ever! I won't let you out of my sight!'

'I thought,' she said very low, 'that you were planning to get married—to Sue?'

'Wrong girl,' he said succinctly. He leaned over her, lifting a strand of her dark hair, smiling down into her eyes with an expression she had never seen there before. The hot sun on their faces, the stillness, it all had a dreamlike quality. But there was nothing dreamlike, she realised the next moment, in Brad's deep tones. 'There's only one girl in the world I want to marry—if she'll have me?' As he spoke he was slipping on her finger a circlet of rubies and diamonds.

'Oh, Brad——!' He read the answer in her eyes and her ardent response to his kiss left no doubts at all.

Harlequin Plus

A WORD ABOUT THE AUTHOR

Born in Western Australia and raised in New Zealand, where she now makes her home, Gloria Bevan has been writing stories of one kind or another for as long as she can remember.

"There is a certain magic about writing," she says enthusiastically, "and I am very happy with my work—even when characters refuse to act the way I want them to!"

Mornings are spent tapping out her thoughts on an ancient typewriter. Afternoons often include the discovery of some exotic destination within short driving distance of her suburban Auckland home. For within an hour or two she can find herself motoring through peach vineyards, happening upon some new golden beach, or visiting an extinct volcano.

Gloria's husband is a building inspector who frequently supplies his author-wife with technical details for her books. They have three grown daughters, each of whom is a devoted fan with her own favorite among "mom's books."

FREE!

**A hardcover Romance Treasury volume
containing 3 treasured works of romance
by 3 outstanding Harlequin authors...**

**...as your introduction to Harlequin's
Romance Treasury subscription plan!**

Romance Treasury

**...almost 600 pages of exciting romance reading
every month at the low cost of $6.97 a volume!**

A wonderful way to collect many of Harlequin's most beautiful love
stories, all originally published in the late '60s and early '70s.
Each value-packed volume, bound in a distinctive gold-embossed
leatherette case and wrapped in a colorfully illustrated dust jacket,
contains...
- 3 full-length novels by 3 world-famous authors of romance fiction
- a unique illustration for every novel
- the elegant touch of a delicate bound-in ribbon bookmark...
  and much, much more!

Romance Treasury

...for a library of romance you'll treasure forever!

Complete and mail today the FREE gift certificate and subscription
reservation on the following page.